The Natural Law

Steve Attridge

© Steve Attridge 2014

Steve Attridge has asserted his rights under the Copyright, Design and Patents Act, 1988, to be identified as the author of this work.

First published in 2014 by Endeavour Press Ltd.

This edition published 2014 by Createspace.

For Neil Marr

Chapter I

'We are all equals in thinking about death, and we all begin and end thinking about it from a position of ignorance... Having no content, we must speak of death metaphorically.'

Jeff Mason

Even as I approached from behind and her head was down looking at something on the laptop, I knew she was trouble. I was right about the nail varnish but hadn't anticipated a blonde. Red handbag, red shoes. If this was a film she would signify danger and sex. Given that it was Marylebone station on a rainy, chilled night, what I could see now as I sat opposite her and she snapped the laptop shut was grief like slashes of sky, etched beneath the make-up and in the lost blue eyes, which also saw menace in everything. The eyes flicked around like nervous little creatures with lives of their own and she couldn't focus. I guessed she had an attention span of about ten seconds, but that was because she was troubled, not stupid.

She'd sent a message to my Rook Investigations website earlier in the day. I felt the familiar twinge of excitement born of fear that is one of my many poisons. An addict of danger despite being something of a coward, I always wonder if this is the one that carves out a road to some new and hopeless derangement of knowledge and pain. *Marylebone station. 6 pm tonight. Victoria and Albert outside tables opposite Burger King. I'll have an open red laptop on the table. MK.* No name, just initials. Why Marylebone? Nice and public but not too big or busy, even at 6 pm. Perhaps it meant they were coming from out of town, like me, and had timed the meeting for trains in and out. Red laptop. Flamboyant. Someone who wants to make a statement, but if they want to do it through the colour of a laptop, they can only be desperate. Red. No, a woman. I made a bet with myself. Twenty pounds says it's a woman, probably with matching red fingernails, perhaps even coat or shoes. A woman with a problem…and a secret. I was right, except for her being blonde.

"You're alone?" she asked.

"Ain't no one here but me and the pigeons."

"You're not what I expected."

"You were expecting a six foot five Puerto Rican with a bandolier of bullets across his naked chest and a sabre scar down one cheek?"

"Just someone better dressed and less exhausted looking. Someone to inspire a bit of confidence. I bet you never take off that greasy old leather jacket."

"I've made a mental note of that and when we next meet I'll wear a Gucci suit and a deep tan. And you're right. I wear this jacket every day. It's the most enduring relationship I've ever had."

She didn't smile. Neither did I. We had yet to unearth something funny and I assumed that whatever she wanted me for would not be a barrel of laughs. I looked at her and calculated.

"Within a three mile radius of the Elephant and Castle. Maybe Blackheath. Left school at sixteen but did...a course in Beauty Care – nails and stuff. Then when the two kids came along you gave it up and anyway there was money coming in so you didn't need to work. But you have aspirations. There's a Dickens novel poking out of your bag. You probably did evening classes. At your local tech."

Now I had her attention, she looked at me properly. Her anxiety level racked up to about six on the Richter scale.

"How did you know who I am?" she asked, surprise overcoming the nest of trouble inside her.

"I don't know who you are. I just know a few things about you."

"I came from Peckham, not Blackheath. And I did evening classes at Goldsmiths. I've since done a lot of things. How did you know I've got two kids?"

"There's a Little Pony sticker on your laptop, so I knew you had a girl, unless you've never grown up, and meeting at six suggests you had post school arrangements to make, and you mentioned Burger King so you knew where it was. You're not a BK girl, but my guess is you have a son who loves it; usually girls prefer Macdonald's. I imagine you waiting for a train while your son tucks into a double cheese."

"Clever patronising sod."

"Sometimes I get things spectacularly wrong. I also know from the way you've been twiddling your wedding ring that all isn't well with your marriage. Your husband missing?"

"He's dead."

"I'm sorry."

I got us coffee and she told me her story. Her name was Mary King. Her husband had been Andy King, a second tier criminal, often the front man for overseas deals – stolen or pirated DVDs, electrical goods, but he'd got a hitch up to the big time, she said, though she didn't know what it was. For once he hadn't felt it was safe to tell her. He'd started to behave oddly – not sleeping, anxious all the time, then he was called to Istanbul, apparently for a business meeting, which was not uncommon, and was found in his hotel room, shot through the head. The day of the funeral Mary received a text. She showed me. *Andy deserved it. Say nothing and I'll leave you and your children alone. Gladiator.* Number unknown. This raised a lot of questions. What was Andy involved in? What had he done to annoy someone to the point of murder? What did Mary know that she should keep to herself? Who was Gladiator? Presumably not Russell Crowe. She had no answers. By talking to me she had probably already put herself in danger. Perhaps she knew something without knowing its significance. After an hour all I had were more questions. She gave me two regular contact names – a Jamaican called Loz and someone who occasionally fenced goods called Jimmy the Stump, due to the fact he had only one hand. She had brought me Andy's address book and a few transit documents for stolen goods. She said he'd done a lot of business in Istanbul recently. I told her to email me details of payments in and out of their bank account for the past year.

She looked at her phone. Time to go.

"It wasn't a marriage made in heaven but it was all I had," she said. "He loved the kids. The dream was to earn a lot for a few years then disappear – I fancied Fiji." A tear rolled down one cheek. I don't go in for grief counselling with clients so I looked down until she recovered.

"I'll make a start. A hundred pounds a day plus expenses. It's cheaper than anyone else but I do my best. Watch your back. If you notice anyone hanging around your house, or if you get calls from someone you don't know contact me. You've got my number?" She didn't have my number, which means she couldn't have given it to anyone else. "One last question. What do you want from this?"

Something hardened in her.

"I just want to know who it was. I want a name for my husband's killer so I can curse it."

Fair enough. I watched her walk away, carrying her little universe of pain. Criminals, and the complicit wives of criminals, are simply people who've made different choices. I often prefer them to the rest of humanity because they have the sniff of danger about them, the simper of secrets. It isn't that I like them; they are just sometimes more interesting to observe. Also, there was always the remote possibility that if my father is still alive, I may come across him. All I know is that he was a middle ranking gang member, mostly warehouse thefts, a few lorry heists. I have a dog eared photograph where he is all shadows but there is the suggestion of a crooked smile. My mother told me nothing when I was growing up, and now she is mostly away with the fairies, so even if she wanted to tell me something it would probably come in a stream of consciousness only those same fairies would comprehend. I must visit her soon.

Before I'd even met Mary King I had a sense something was about to happen. It's like a buzzing in the ears. You can't see the bug but you know it's there in the dark, near, and that it means you harm. Senses heighten, things accrue significance. For me it began with looking at a car crash. Everything connects eventually.

Chapter II

'Where there is mystery, it is generally suspected there must also be evil.'

Bertolt Brecht

The car seems to make up its own mind. A blood red jaguar bored with the monotony of traffic breaks ranks, and increases speed as it careers across to the lanes of oncoming traffic, spilling a helmeted cyclist who cartwheels through the air like a kicked beetle. A terrified woman yanks back her pram before the car vaults the pavement, now apparently determined to launch into the Thames propelled by a twin turbo death wish. The front buckles as it slams the wall, a lurch of metal and rubber as it takes the impact, the driver's white head smacking into the windscreen and bouncing back. The head breaks; the glass does not even crack. Bullet-proof. Probably the whole car is armoured against imaginary attacks, all at taxpayers expense, supported by the erroneous conviction that a politician's life is worth more than the rest of us. Hugh Dillsburgh, MP for somewhere in the shires and big cheese in the Foreign Office. RIP. I wondered what would happen to the car. Even after a rip like this it would be worth the collective annual salaries of ten sheet metal workers.

"Dad, how many more times are you going to watch that crash? You're weird."

Cass, my beloved daughter, my avocation, my palliative and occasional torment, sat on the sofa in my cramped living room, looking at me with her ruminating mix of bewilderment, love and approbation. Living with me off and on, alternating between maternal concern and childish horror at my own car crash of a life, our love burns bright in the darkness between us. Since she discovered my double life, philosophy lecturer by day, Rook Investigations by inclination, I had not so much risen in her esteem as cracked the grid by which she could measure me. I was simply a father, fact. I was also, bizarrely, her university tutor and tomorrow morning I would enter my office, ten minutes late, to begin her 2nd year option course on Natural Law. I tried to work out how, given that I had no desire to teach the unteachable to a bunch of debt ridden teenagers, even if Cass was one of them, I could end the session early. I am as passionate about ideas as I am dispassionate about teaching.

I stopped the YouTube film of the crash, helpfully captured by some passer-by on their iPhone. The official mainstream news, never to be trusted, said he had suffered a fatal heart attack. He would be loved and missed by all. A man of remarkable abilities and abundant integrity. A sure sign he was probably a weasel of the first order, but I am biased and have an ulterior motive for watching this little drama on a loop. Dear old Hugh was the boss of David, my former best friend and now my ex-wife's lover. I kept watching in the ludicrous hope that David would suddenly appear in the car, and would die as horribly as his beloved boss. We are all creators of our own life scripts and are infuriated when our central role is suddenly usurped, when our desires are thwarted, and we realise we are not the author of our lives at all, but, like Prufrock, a bit part, a footman to our own passing time, a pair of ragged claws. And so it was, David Hills, MP and dipshit of the first order, remained annoyingly intact, and would no doubt at this moment be cradling a glass of Merlot in one hand and my ex-wife Lizzie's breast in the other as he launched into a sanctimonious dribble of lamenting grief, while secretly hoping that the now very vacant diplomatic post would drop greasily into his open paws. I often find that if you think the worst of people, you are rarely disappointed. However, I was already asking other questions. Did the glorious Hugh have a history of heart problems? Why wasn't he wearing a seat belt? Did he normally drive himself? Would anyone else ask them? Probably not.

Then I got the message from Mary King. After talking to her I decided to see Jimmy the Stump first. I planned to go the next day. Before that I had to show my face at the university. In my department changes were abounding with all the excitement of having a wart removed. New scents. The dying air beating feebly with new blood. I had successfully engineered a complete nervous breakdown for my Head of Department, Jeremy Tregown, a bitter and incomplete man who underestimated his nemesis – me. Someone should have warned him to go quietly into that goodnight of academic obscurity and not seek conflicts for which he was entirely unfitted. He was neither generous nor gifted and I feel no remorse. I wandered down the corridor when the new Head of Department's door opened. Audrey Pritchard, Professor of Social Something-not-very-interesting, white startled hair, anaemic and bowelled, squinty, wet lips, a hint of the Georgian fop about her. She smiled, her mouth like cooing baby eels.

"Dr. Rook, hail fellow well met. A minute of your time."

"I'm late for my seminar," I smiled back.

"Then you'll be a minute later," she said, and I entered her inner sanctum. It was a scary cave of graphs and charts and numbers sanctified by a few posters of Suffragettes.

"Your reputation goes before you and, as we both know, a reputation is a dangerous thing," she said, still smiling.

"I have a reputation?"

"For going your own sweet way. For being cavalier. A law unto yourself."

"Who would have thought?"

"And I just wanted to say how much I admire those qualities. And wouldn't it be a salutary thing if we could harness them to enhance the profile of the department? Which is why I've drawn up this." She produced a neatly printed sheet of A4 with my name at the top and next to it the ominous phrase: 'TARGET SHEETS FOR AUTUMN SEMESTER'. "You'll see I've given you a pleasing range and balance of targets for the next three months. Purely academic, administrative and pastoral. I want you to find yourself in these challenges. I'll be monitoring them closely and my door is always open."

I glanced at my next three months. One conference paper, a book proposal, designing a distance learning module and I was also to be PDP (Personal Development Plan) Staff Tutor.

"I've taken the liberty of calling your first Staff PDP meeting on Friday at 5.30 pm. We don't want it cutting into the ordinary working day, do we? Anything you'd like to ask?"

"Yes, more of a request, really."

She continued smiling.

"Could you stop smiling? It has associations of dementia. Hospitals. Cabbage. Decay."

Battle lines had been drawn. I got to my office and then couldn't face it. The salt had gone from me. I opened the door and a dozen fresh faces turned.

"Cancelled. Afraid the new Head of Department insists I count paper clips for the next two hours. Think about the following: what is the relationship between what is good and what is right in theories of Natural Law?"

Cass looked at me and shook her head wearily.

In the car park I took a few deep breaths of suburban chill and got in my ancient Saab. I thought I would cold call on Jimmy. Sometimes if people know you're coming they prepare what to say. I like to catch them off guard sometimes. During the drive I amused myself with plotting the perfect murder so that David would be out of my life forever and Lizzie, my beloved ex, crystal woman of my whisky dreams, would grieve and I would comfort her with honeyed words and wine, and we would dissolve out of our clothes into bed and all would be restored, and the myriad complex brutalities of betrayal and the thousand small shocks that weaken love and ache the flesh would be gone in the darkness of an eternal night.

My phone bleated and I read a new text: *Marylebone. Good meeting? So it begins. Gladiator.* Number unknown. Only Cass could have known about my meeting, unless someone had hacked my laptop, and that had never happened before. I had every firewall and viral protection known to man and machine. And why were they so interested? I had barely started this investigation and already someone was monitoring me, presumably the same person who contacted Mary King and probably killed her husband.

*

Jimmy lived near Baker Street in a tall red brick building of apartments. I rang and said on the intercom that I was a friend of Andy King's. He buzzed me in. I walked up two flights of grim stairs that smelled of sour milk and rotten vegetables. He opened the door and looked me up and down, then stood aside and I entered a world of birds.

In the small living room there were over fifty cages, with budgerigars, canaries, macaws, small grey parrots, and many varieties I couldn't recognise, but all watchful, chirruping, bobbing on perches, hitting tiny bells with their heads, looking crazily in mirrors. There must have been sixty birds in the little room. I started to count but they kept moving and I stopped eventually at fifty eight. A dozen or so green and blue budgies clung to the curtains and one flew up to me and perched on my shoulder.

"Griselda. She likes you. Must be your smell. Usually she hides from strangers."

I knew from the din that the adjoining rooms were also full of birds. The Bird Man of Bakerloo. I could see why. Living in a city gives you the illusion of movement and life, whereas in reality you are a brick in the wall. The birds gave him a promise of flight, a dream of escape, but despite the cacophony of twitters and cheeps and the abundance of feathery life, it depressed me. Caged birds give me the jitters. I can't breathe. My throat closes and I want to free them, then run with them until they are safely skywards and free of the world, until some predator bites off their head. I'm the same with zoos, now politely called bio parks or conservation parks, but still a place where you cage wild creatures and charge people to gawp at them. As much as Jimmy clearly loved these birds, from looking around the room I could see abnormalities, such as repetitive behaviour; a blue-green budgie head weaves back and forth, another shifts constantly from one foot to the other; there was obsessive grooming in which several birds were plucking out their own feathers, and aggressive behaviour as two singing canaries cheeped harmoniously then tried to peck a lump from each other. Things caged diminish me. I'd rather take my chances in the jungle than die quietly in the airport lounge.

"Kettle's boiled. Sugar?"

"No thanks," I said. I noticed two mugs already on the table. A little Toby jug of milk. It was as if he had been expecting me. He was.

"My name's..."

"Paul Rook. Private Investigator. Bit of a philosopher too."

It's not often I'm surprised. How the hell did he know who I was and that I was going to visit? I didn't know myself until half an hour ago. He looked at my confusion. A pretty translucent green bird perched on the biscuit barrel he was about to open.

"You rang, Mister Rook. Or rather, it was a landline phone message. About twenty minutes ago and told me you were coming. I wouldn't forget, not with a name like yours. Rook – or *Corvus frugilegus*, member of the Corvidae family in the passerine order of birds. Named by Carl Linnaeus in 1758. Intelligent. Ka-ah Ka-ah. Distinctive call. Good at working things out, solving problems to get what it wants. You know, in an experiment, a rook was put near a tube of water, with a worm floating on the water surface, and some stones next to the tube. The water level was too low for the rook to reach the worm, so it placed stones in the tube until the level was high enough to get the worm. Is something wrong?"

Yes. Everything was wrong.

Chapter III

'It is the dim haze of mystery that adds
enchantment to pursuit.'
Joseph Joubert

Jimmy reiterated that I had telephoned him. Unless I was going the way of my mother and each second was a fresh universe of unmeaning and mystery without memory or arrangement, someone was toying with me, and showing me they were in control. The text, and now this. I let it go for the moment. Jimmy was surprisingly open; usually criminals tell me nothing until they know I'm not a threat, but he chatted amiably as a smallish green parrot with an orange beak and a whitish grey ringed breast, as if he was wearing a vest, scuttled along his perch and screeched lines from *The Charge of the Light Brigade*:

"Half a league, half a league,

Half a league onward,
All in the valley of Death
Rode the six hundred."

Jimmy smiled indulgently; I realised these birds were all his sons and daughters in the odd brew of his imagination. He wore a black leather glove where a right hand should be.

"Loves Tennyson, so I called him Alfred. Knows every line. Amazing little fellow. A quaker parrot. Smart talkers. Fertile brains, parrots. Need constant stimulation otherwise they get restless and bored. Always liked the quaker. He's got a vocab of over five hundred words. Now, Andy King. Nice lad but shall we say incautious. Breezy. Thought everything would turn out right as nine pence if he kept smiling. Bit of a peacock – all feathers and no brain. He'd be the one who wouldn't see the cat coming."

The parrot was unstoppable:

"Cannon to right of them,
Cannon to left of them,
Cannon in front of them
Volleyed and thundered;"

I finished the verse for him:

"Stormed at with shot and shell,
Boldly they rode and well,
Into the jaws of Death,
Into the mouth of hell
Rode the six hundred."

The parrot stopped and eyed me, his head moving to one side. Then he flew from his perch and sat on my shoulder. He started to nibble my ear lobe, clucking softly, one dark intelligent eye a bite away from mine. Jimmy beamed.

"You stole his thunder. Alfred likes an educated person. Not many of those come round here. Remember this about parrots. If they go still and pin you with an eye they're getting ready to bite."

"Andy King," I reminded him.

"Andy King," echoed Alfred the parrot.

"I was sorry to hear. He'd got involved in something and he was dying to tell me, but was afraid to. I had a phone call a while back asking if I'd vouch for him. I did and got five hundred quid for it. I don't know what it was but it was a step up. I got the feeling he was watching his back."

"Who phoned you?"

"Never got a name."

"What do you think he was into?"

Jimmy shrugged. "He was killed in Istanbul, right?"

"Yes."

"What do you think he was doing in Istanbul?"

"I think it was a stopover."

"Right. Could be India."

"Or it could be Afghanistan. Andy wasn't political?"

Jimmy smiled.

"If you mentioned right or left wing he'd think you were talking football."

"Security?"

"Didn't have the background. Listen, I'll ask around. Andy was liked. He had a good mate called Rod…what is it? Whyley or Riley. It'll come. Ring me tomorrow and I'll let you know what I've found out."

At least I knew a little more about Andy King than I had when I arrived.

*

I went for a coffee and thought about death. We rarely see it coming, but what if we could, as when you know you have a fatal illness? Did Andy King see it coming? What had he done to bring it about? Montaigne wrote an essay: 'That to Philosophise is to Learn to Die'. He considers Cicero's idea that to study philosophy is to learn to die, because quiet thought and contemplation create stillness, a movement away from the world, which is a simulacrum of death, but in doing that we learn not to fear death, and in turn may learn to appreciate life more. By knowing death we can live better. It quietens something in us.

I walked to Regents Park, just stepping onto the train when I got a text: *You have pulled the lever. Will you take responsibility? Gladiator*. Number Unknown. What the hell? Somebody was still watching, and playing games. Two stops later the message thundered home. How could I be so slow?

Pulling the lever is a reference to the trolley problem – an ethical philosophical dilemma. There are five people tied to a railway track and a trolley is thundering towards them. You are standing next to a lever and can divert the trolley to another line where one person is tied. What do you do? A utilitarian would say you choose the one person to die. An alternative view is that by doing anything you are actively participating in a situation where moral crimes are already in place. It gets more convoluted than that, but you get the point. What had I done? I'd just been to see Jimmy and perhaps merely by doing that I'd pulled a lever in events. It seemed to take an age before the train stopped. I ran upstairs and couldn't find my oyster card, so hurdled the barrier, nearly broke my ankle and ran up the steps with a station guard running behind me and shouting. In the road I jumped in a taxi, next to an elderly woman wearing a white leather coat, a black hat and enough perfume to furnish a brothel.

"Emergency," I said.

"How delightful. Where are we going?" she said, smiling through a landslide of pan make-up.

"To see if a family of birds is intact," I said.

"Marvellous," she said.

Ten minutes later we pulled up outside the block. How long was it since I was there? Fifty minutes? What could have happened? I got out of the cab and ran across the road. A little boy was looking up and pointing and laughing. Way up a window was open and a cascade of birds flying out, painting the dull brickwork, slate roof and grey sky with alarming colour. Blues, greens, reds, yellows, fluttering wings. Cries and squawks. A line of budgerigars perched on the sill. Another line on the roof, bobbing their heads and chattering in their new and shocking freedom. A pigeon sat fatly on a window ledge and watched this exotic exodus. Damn damn damn, I kept ringing Jimmy's number on the brass plate but no answer. I rang the flat below. A woman answered.

"Police. We suspect an intruder. Please buzz me in and stay inside with your door locked." The door buzzed. The lift was on the fifth so I took the stairs three at a time. A breathless twenty seconds later Jimmy's door wasn't locked and I ran in. I knew before I saw him. He lay on the floor, his face swollen and the colour of putty, clusters of tiny veins broken on his cheeks. He'd been garrotted. In the Middle Ages, garrotting was a means of execution for someone who was to be burned at the stake, but who had 'confessed' their heresy and so was spared the long agony of the flames. Then the lifeless body was burned.

There was also a horrible sponge like wound on his head the shape of a crescent moon where he'd presumably cracked his head as he fell, or tried to struggle. Blood oozed thickly and was already congealing and darkening. It's not easy to garrotte someone and this person knew what they were doing, probably a thin wire one to judge by the wound. One handless arm was across his chest, the other on a chair as if he'd tried to lever himself up while he was dying.

A pretty lemon coloured canary, bright as a small sun, sat on his chest and cheeped quizzically. A blue and green budgerigar sat by his head, gently pecking his chin as if trying to awaken him. I put my ear to his chest. Felt for a pulse. Nothing. He was gone. A pandemonium of birds all around, though many had flown out. I wondered if something of Jimmy had flown with them. Cages were upturned and most had been opened. Why would someone who had just killed Jimmy let all these birds go? Presumably he'd been killed because he'd talked to me, and might have more to say, but the birds had played no part in it.

I closed the windows and sat until the thought came – the cages and windows were opened before Jimmy died. This made sense. Jimmy loved them more than he did himself, so what better way to make him confess what he'd told me than to release into an uncertain world and probable death the things he loved? The little he'd told me was not worth this death, not worth something that came creeping sly and malevolent, a dark thing in a corner waiting to happen and work its grubby purpose. Much as I hated their imprisonment, the birds had endeared him to me. I liked the incongruity of it, of him. I was sorry.

I put on gloves and made a quick search of the room. A mock antique roll top desk revealed only bills and correspondence with various bird organizations. I pocketed his address book. I checked his telephone to get the last number rang and copied it. I froze with the receiver in my hand. A sound. A muffled word. Someone was in the flat with me. It could only be the killer. I looked around for a weapon and picked up a long silver paper knife. My hands were clammy inside the gloves. Then again. A breath. A murmur. From the kitchen. I stepped up and slowly started to open the door. Much to my annoyance I was excited. It was one of many things warped in my little inner world. Some piece of machinery gone askew. Then a voice.

"Don't hit me, please, don't hit me. I haven't said anything. I don't know anything. Just go away. Please."

I looked down at Jimmy, growing colder by the minute, yet there was his voice coming from the kitchen. And I knew. It could only be. I opened the door further and there was Alfred, sitting on the kitchen table. He took a grape from a bowl and nibbled it, then swallowed, did a little jig to a chair back and looked at me, head cocked to one side.

"I haven't said anything. I don't know anything. Just go away. Please. No, no," he said in a perfect and ridiculously moving simulation of Jimmy's voice.

I would have to revise my ideas about death. The dead may be gone but their voices live on, albeit in a parrot, himself perhaps a reincarnation of Alfred Lord Tennyson.

"What else do you know, Alfred? What else did you hear?" I asked.

He threw back his head and gave an ear piercing shriek. Then a groan. Silence.

Chapter IV

'Friendship is the greatest of all.'
Seneca

I stopped and telephoned the police anonymously from a public phone, and said they would also need someone to take care of a lot of birds. As I drove back I planned my next move: to trace Andy King's bank payments, because if you follow the money it sometimes starts to tell a story. I'd also go to see Jamaican Loz. Presumably Andy King's killer also murdered Jimmy, but what or who was he protecting? I tried the last number Jimmy rang and got an anonymous answerphone, so stopped the call. I looked at the passenger seat. Alfred sat in a cage looking solemnly and curiously at the road ahead. I assumed he hadn't been out in a while and had a lot of new sensory input to process. He'd obviously heard and seen all that happened in the flat and might tell me more. Besides, I liked him. I went to the university to put up some 'seminar cancelled' notices. I put Alfred on my desk and suddenly realised he was a big responsibility. What did he eat – grapes apart? Could I let him out of the cage at all? How often did his cage need cleaning? What other needs did he have?

Mrs Simpson, one of the few people in the university I can tolerate, entered with her mop and bucket. In the bucket was a chilled bottle of Sancerre; she'd obviously seen me arriving. She gave a little gasp.

"Oh my blimey, it's a quaker. Hello there," she said smiling and approached the cage.

Alfred eyed her, then did a little jig. She put her hand to the cage and he nibbled her finger very gently and rolled an eye at her. I swear he was flirting.

"You know about parrots?" I asked.

"My old dad kept a few. Intelligent things they are."

"*Into the valley of death rode the six hundred,*" said Alfred, and followed it with an ear shredding wolf whistle.

Within ten minutes we'd done a deal. I gave her some money to buy food for Alfred. She'd check on him whenever I wasn't here, which was most of the time, and she'd spend her breaks and lunch times with him and change his water. I had no doubt that within a few days he'd have a juicy gossip map of the whole campus. Jez, a night security guard friend of hers, would keep an eye on him overnight. He'd probably be better off than in my tiny flat with long periods of being alone. I didn't know what a Pandora's Box Alfred would open during the next week.

When Mrs Simpson left I started to trace Andy King's bank statements. He had been getting heavy duty payments from a company called Ocean Investments. It had associations of health, fresh air, new horizons. It wasn't registered at Companies House. There was a box number in London, another in Prague, and nothing else.

I had an email from the ghastly Audrey Pritchard, reminding me that tomorrow was Friday and I was to chair the first PDP meeting. I hacked into the Staff Counsellor's hard drive to see if there was any useful information on Audrey – any psychological tics, personal problems, emotional baggage, that I could use as leverage if needs must, but there was nothing. Unless Audrey was hiding something, she was inanely, annoyingly normal. Tomorrow could take care of itself.

I looked at Alfred and he stared back, his head to one side.

"There was another name. Rod Whyley or Riley. I wonder if Jimmy ever remembered," I said.

"The name's Whiteley. Rod Whiteley. Must give that Rook fella a bell later," said Alfred in Jimmy's voice. So he *had* remembered.

I smiled.

"Good lad. See you tomorrow, Alfred."

He bobbed his head up and down, eyes like black stars.

"Forward, the Light Brigade!"

Was there a man dismay'd?
Not tho' the soldier knew
Some one had blunder'd."
I finished the verse.
"Theirs not to make reply,
Theirs not to reason why,
Theirs but to do and die.
Into the valley of Death
Rode the six hundred."
I was starting to really like Alfred.

*

I don't go in for close friendships, apart from Cass, and Lizzie at one time; I prefer my own company. Given that my best friend David had been slyly shafting my wife while still being my best friend, allow me a few barbs of cynicism. One day I will probably kill him. In 301 BC Epicurus maintained that wisdom tells us that the greatest facilitator of happiness is the possession of friendship. The argument runs that others who care for us confirm our identities, and are more likely to understand what we say. I say that happiness is vastly overrated and a logical impossibility to attain as a permanent state. I concur with Paul Valéry's dictum that "God created man and, finding him not sufficiently alone, gave him a companion to make him feel his solitude more keenly." Aloneness is authentic. It's where our real work is done in the crucible of the human.

However, when I was in my teens and early twenties I did have a soul mate, Symon Crace, a fellow renegade soul who, like me, spent all his spare time chasing his own demons, only for them to return sturdier. We were the brothers neither of us had, both smart, self-destructive and contradictory. We each loved philosophy but, after university, he joined the civil service, then left to start his own business. We kept in touch but after a few years I was married, entrenched in academia and he was a globetrotting executive with a successful trading company, mostly minerals and gold. I hadn't seen him in ten years, but when I opened the door to my flat, there was the familiar lopsided smile, the flick of blonde hair flecked with grey now, his body a little heavier, cradling a glass of my Rioja, and making Cass laugh.

"Paul. God you look terrible. Much older than I do. What on earth has life done to you?"

"And you. Look how enormous you are. Elephantine. Business lunches and no angst to thin you. I thought you were Oliver Hardy in a blonde wig."

An hour of banter and drinking. Cass clearly enjoyed his company and thought it good for me. She went out wherever daughters go when they want to worry their fathers, and Symon produced a bottle of Longmorn 1992 Malt Whisky, ninety pounds a bottle. An hour later it was three quarters gone, as was I, and Symon had told me his story. His trading company had started to make rollercoaster profits when the recession hit and people started buying gold. He brokered a US-China deal that minted his bank account and he woke up one morning realising that he need never work again. He sold the company at a huge profit and started travelling, and was now contemplating what to do with the rest of his life. No family. He said he'd become increasingly less interested in the amount of money he'd acquired and had already given a substantial amount away to an anti-gun lobby in the States. I asked why that in particular and he said an employee of his in the Michigan office had been shot walking home, and somehow he felt responsible. It was ridiculous but guilt is an irrational goblin of the night.

I almost told him about my other life, but even the whisky couldn't loosen my tongue that much. I cleared out my broom cupboard of a study, threw down a camp bed and before I'd brushed my teeth and wondered what colour my hangover would be tomorrow I could hear him gently snoring. It was good to see him. Almost a relief, as if the past had appeared to validate itself and me with it. Nostalgia is mostly a foreign country to me, but the combination of Symon and a bottle of whisky lifted the portcullis and all manner of madnesses cascaded through.

I rang Lizzie.

"It's me," I said. Not the most scintillating opening line.

"It's one in the morning," she said.

"It was your ability to tell the time that first made me fall in love with you."

"You're drunk."

"Of course I am, otherwise I wouldn't be ringing you to say that I still love you and will parade naked and shivering through the streets of Watford, flagellating myself with a toilet brush, in an attempt to win back your heart, but mostly your naked body."

She hung up. I fell into a dark sleep and had a dream about my father. He was standing over my bed and I looked up at the shadow and said, "Just let me see your face properly. Just once." He said, "You'd only regret it." The night caved in around me and I had a whisky sleep of turmoil and damage, the world shape-changing like a turbulent ocean that carried only indifferent violence in its heart.

I looked a hundred years old in the morning, a fact confirmed by Cass as she gave me a mug of coffee and two aspirin.

"How long is he staying?" she asked.

"Not long, I'd imagine," I said, my tongue trying not to strangle the words in its puffed misery. She looked at me smugly. "What?" I asked.

"It's just that it's a bit of a first. You enjoying someone's company. You do realise you have a seminar on Free Will this morning?"

"Cass, I want you to put up a cancelled notice for me. I'm busy this morning. And ask Mrs Simpson if Alfred is OK."

"Who's Alfred?"

"I'm sharing my office with him."

"But you never share an office. You hate your colleagues."

"Alfred's alright. Take in a few grapes for him."

I left her baffled and stumbled out into the grey misery of an English autumn.

Chapter V

'Those who are easily shocked should be shocked more often.'

Mae West

I found Loz playing an old fashioned flipper machine in an amusement arcade in Marine Parade in Southend. The drive down had done nothing to clear my head, but three coffees had made me twitchy and anxious. I counted four hundred and sixteen red cars and two hundred and twenty eight white cars on the way down. Don't ask me why. I just count things. My mother used to bring me to Southend for caravan holidays when I was a child. The caravans always smelt damp and cabbagey, the communal toilets made me gag, but it nevertheless seemed incongruously exotic to me simply to be near the sludge-grey sea. We would trudge outside and put sticks in the ground and play Ashes – I would be England and she Australia and she always let me win. I must go and see her. Loz was late thirties, tall, black, rangy, cool in an exhausted way, and didn't even look up when I introduced myself and mentioned Andy King. He slapped the flippers and the silver ball jangled and banged its course until it disappeared in a small hole.

It was a gamble coming to see him. My talking to Jimmy had cost him his life. Did that mean Loz would be at risk too? I thought that perhaps the killer would feel he'd made his point and frightened me off. Perhaps he'd just got lucky in anticipating me going to see Jimmy. Also, what he didn't know is that the possibility of being stalked was making me buzz. I thought Loz would be safe.

"Yuh gat a cigarette?" he asked.

"No, but I'll buy you a pack if you take a stroll with me."

We walked along the pier, with the depressed paintwork and down at heel engineering of Adventure Island on the left – a rollercoaster covered with a tarpaulin looking like a mummified caterpillar. English seaside places at their worst are depressing and at their best have a beautiful melancholy about them. They are places for children and the elderly to live, and the rest of us to visit. Reaching the end I looked down at the wash of the Atlantic like a swirling bowl of dirty washing up water. Loz flicked his cigarette into the whorl. I knew what he was waiting for and gave him fifty pounds.

"Andy think he a player but he jus' a hustler. He was a OK mon and we did some bizniz togetha but then he get some offer. Bandulu bizness. All I know is it was heavy. Prob'ly whole heap drugs. Coke. Speed. H. Who knows? I jus' know someone told mi nah to get involved."

"Who?"

"Just a text. Anonymous. From some mutha call hisself Gla-di-a-tor. Y'know? Wha the fuck? I listen. Smalltime crooking nobody botha but I dohn want to mix wid bad people no more. I was in de army. I dohn want nuh mo of this." He lifted his shirt and there was a raw looking scar where he'd taken a bullet. "Iraq. Whole place a ugly fuckup."

He didn't have much else to add. We walked back down the pier and I said goodbye. I got in my car and watched him walk away, presumably to the amusement arcade. I got a text, this time from a numbered mobile: *Loz's life – the crocodile paradox. What's your answer? No answer and he definitely dies. Try to block me and I kill you both. Gladiator.* I looked up and could still see Loz. I got out of the car and ran towards him but stopped when I saw the little flickering red dot on his back. Someone had a gun trained on him with red dot sight. I looked behind me but could only see cars, houses, a bus. It could be long range. If he was a good shot he could be out of vision. If I stood to block the red dot we'd both die. A rapid fire weapon can take out a small crowd in seconds.

The crocodile paradox is a puzzle in logic. A crocodile steals a child, and promises the father that his son will be returned only if he can correctly predict whether or not the crocodile will return the child. If the father guesses that the child will be returned and he's right then all may be well. However, the crocodile is in a dilemma if the father guesses the child will not be returned. If the father is right then the child must be returned, but then the father's prediction is falsified. It's a logical maze and only has meaning if the crocodile is honest about his original intention. You get the idea? I was being asked to predict whether or not the texter was going to kill Loz. Given the killer's previous form it seemed logical that he would kill Loz, but I gambled on the opposite because one of the things I already knew about the killer was that he had a knack for the unpredictable. I texted back: *You won't kill him because you've already made your point.*

I looked at the ambling unaware figure of Loz and the faint red flicker still danced on his back. If I shouted to warn him I had no doubt he'd be shot. I looked behind again, then down at my phone. *Correct. This number no longer exists.* Loz turned into the arcade. This person was psychotic and even had a bizarre integrity. What next? I tried ringing the number but it had vapoured into the ether. I wrote it in my notebook anyway.

I drove around for half an hour but saw nothing and no one. He'd had his fun and now was gone. The killer had intensified my problem. I could only find out what had happened to Andy King by talking to people, but the mere act of talking to them put them in mortal danger. The killer could only know who I was going to see by either following me, or being frighteningly prescient. He was making me culpable, trying to force me into taking responsibility for the lives of others, and in doing this creating a bond between us. In his own mind we now shared the murders. Not killing Loz was a baroque way of telling me that he was a just god in that he kept his word. I was just about to drive off when I got another text, this time from an unknown number: *Eventually everything connects. HDJMMK. I'll call you later. Gladiator.* I recognised the first phrase as something said by Charles Eames. He and his brother Ray were designers who had a powerful philosophy of design and Charles believed that people, ideas and objects all eventually connect in some elaborate pattern or configuration. The capital letters meant nothing to me. I puzzled over them as I drove back. I was excited. It was amoral now that lives were involved, but that's also what buzzed me. I rationalised that I had taken this job and was a long way from seeing it through.

*

I had the damned meeting to chair at the University. When I arrived in my office Alfred was out of his cage, on a perch nibbling a piece of apple.

"Hi Alfred. How was your day?"

He cocked his head to one side and said, "Blimey, you're a comedian," in a perfect imitation of Mrs. Simpson's voice. I sat at my desk while Alfred finished his apple, then he fluttered onto my shoulder, nibbled my ear, and watched as I switched on my PC. Five minutes later a knock at the door heralded the arrival of four dismal colleagues. Two women and two men. One of the women, dressed for a wake, was clearly looking for a fight. I asked them to sit down.

"Why have you got a parrot on your shoulder?" asked the wake lady.

"Because there wasn't room on the desk," I said.

"They carry diseases," she said.

"We all do that," I said.

There were a few desultory jokes about Long John Silver, then I called them to order. I already had my TM plan. TM doesn't stand for transcendental meditation but for Truncate Meeting.

"What I'd like is for everyone to give a detailed outline of their research plans for the next year, which I will write down and log with the Head of Department. Also an off-the-top-of-your-head reading list for a new MA in Interdisciplinary Critical Thinking."

They all looked blank. So far so good.

"No one? Perhaps you all need a little more time to prepare."

The relief was visible. You could almost smell it. They shuffled out, except Ron. I always forget about Ron. Fifty something, nondescript, a walking shadow. Someone life failed to notice, as if he slipped through the net of things, an unoccupied shell who ghosted down corridors and through rooms. I neither liked nor disliked him. He was the sort of person to excite extreme indifference. Even Alfred seemed bored and hopped off my shoulder and started cakewalking along my desk and muttering obscenities to himself.

"What is it, Ron? I'm busy."

"I just thought that now you're PD Tutor, we could have a little chat."

"But what could we possibly have to say to each other?"

"It's just, I have a few problems. Eight years in psychotherapy. There are several things about my childhood that perhaps we could tease out together. You're a philosopher. You might have the bigger picture. Students sense my low self-worth. I'm sure that's why they ignore everything I say. What do you think, Paul? I mean – I'd like you to be honest."

"No you wouldn't, Ron."

Alfred shrieked with laughter.

"I would. I admire honesty."

"No, you don't. No one does. Honesty creates chaos and heartache."

"Try me," said Ron, striking a pathetically dramatic pose.

I made a snap decision. Clearly certain unscrupulous people had been killing Ron with kindness for years. He needed an emergency infusion of reality. If he survived he might even thank me.

"OK. I wish you could be me just for two minutes, then you'd see for yourself what a crashing bore you are. You've wasted years of your life and salary on a succession of witch doctor therapists who are more than happy to feed the illusion that you are a complicated man with interesting problems. You're not. Here's twenty quid. Just go and get drunk is my advice."

I left and puzzled further on the text I'd received. I had a few hours before the killer telephoned.

Chapter VI

'Nature adheres to an immutable order; humanity to an ever-increasing chaos…Don't shrink from nature's brutal perfection. Take joy in it. Embrace it.'

Boyd Rice

I called in to see Anna on the way back. She is a sometimes lover and likes it when I call in unexpectedly and we go straight to bed. She has a generous body, an open mind and a distinctive take on things. Sex is the equivalent of an adrenalin inducing run or serious retail therapy for her, a thrill among others but with no special value. She thinks herself a free spirit, but I think her attachment to freedom is itself a form of imprisonment, and her fear of not being free itself cages her. Her chains rattle even as she denies them. Her complete lack of curiosity about the lives of others is perhaps because she fears that knowledge of them will trammel her and bog down sex with baggage she spends her life fiercely resisting. I say none of this, but I asked her once if she would mind if she never saw me again. She said she would wish me well but the waters would close almost instantly, so it suits us both because my heart is always elsewhere.

The smooth terrace of her spine, the genius of her breasts, her hungry thighs, are only reminders of another, lost body, that of my wife. My lovemaking with Anna is complicit with the death of love. The body always betrays the heart, its own rhythms and desires chirrup mockingly at the absence of the beloved. It seems to me that desire is always about what you have already lost. Anna would not mind knowing this; it would amuse her. Perhaps she too thinks of others, but for her the lovers blur into some formless dream of desire. I celebrate the apple wood smell of her hair, the voyeuristic enthusiasms of her desires, the dimples in her lower back, the clutch of her legs and arch of her spine as she climaxes, and the way she would smile at these comments I now make. In time we could become just friends and I would value her thoughts on the blurred colours of my life.

Anna's flat is like her life: uncluttered, no personal items proclaim a history or attachments. As if her life is full of unidentified spaces which others occupy temporarily and she acknowledges each in passing, but none with longing, regret or affinity. She is a vessel of strangers. I am amazed at the remoteness of her passion, the warm indifference of her intimacies. Erotically futureless. She is there but not present, as if we live in a mirror and her essential life is somewhere else. She does not encourage too much conversation, so I am free to have these thoughts.

As I left her flat I felt a chill. As if I was being watched, which perhaps I was. The killer would telephone me later – I knew he would keep his word because there was something Newtonian about him. Fixed. He had a sense that with the right information and secrecy the universe would run like clockwork, but it probably doesn't. He thinks he is in control, and the truth is – no one is.

When I got home there was the unfamiliar sound of laughter. Cass was giggling as Symon told her a story about a former business colleague who got hiccoughs whenever he was lying during negotiations. We ate some pasta and a carrot and nut salad that Symon had prepared. It was annoyingly delicious, and Cass kept complimenting him.

"Why don't you learn to cook, Dad?" she asked.

"His mind's always on higher things," said Symon, smiling at me.

"Speaking of which, a puzzle," I said.

I wrote down the letters HDJMMK. They both looked.

"Not an anagram. No vowels," said Cass.

"Some sort of code. What's the context?" asked Symon.

Cass looked at me. She guessed it was to do with an investigation and wondered if I would tell Symon, but I said nothing. Secrecy serves me well.

I said it had been given to me by a student. We puzzled over it. An abbreviation for something, but what? Were the letters cryptically alluding to something or did they have an intrinsic meaning? We tried various cryptographic possibilities, substitution and transposition ciphers, numerical matches. Nothing came.

I went to my bedroom, now doubling as my study, and left Cass and Symon to a game of chess. I looked at the text again: *Eventually everything connects. HDJMMK. I'll call you later. Gladiator.* The letters connected, but how? The phone rang – unknown number. I answered but said nothing. Just white noise.

"It's you, isn't it?" I said, pressing the *record* button.

"Shut up and listen." A digitally encrypted voice to disguise the real one. It sounded like Darth Vader with a cold. "You've done well, or should I say we've done well. The crocodile problem could have gone either way, but Loz wasn't relevant. You want to know why I'm doing this. The answer is simple: I have to. And don't tell me I don't. It's Natural Law. You want to know who's next, but what's in a name? I have to go. I'm about to enter a busy period. A royal goodbye to you."

And the call stopped. I listened to it three times. What was he telling me? This wasn't a courtesy call. Whoever he was he had an oblique purpose because I knew by now I was dealing with a psychotic mind that always had an ulterior motive. As I'd surmised, he now saw me as an accomplice. He feels he has no choices in the path he's following – that he is being driven by something – God, fate, his own genes. 'What's in a name?' is a phrase from Romeo and Juliet – was he using the romantic tragedy to tell me something? And a royal goodbye – why royal? By mentioning his next victim it seemed he had a hit list irrespective of who I contacted. Perhaps I still put people in danger but I was the only one who could possibly prevent further carnage by finding and stopping the killer. It was a moral quagmire. I was both inside and outside his web.

I went back into the lounge where Cass was just checkmating Symon, but I knew from his smile that he'd let her win. If she knew she'd call him a patronising bastard, but at that moment her triumph overrode her intuition. The TV was on and there was a piece about Hugh Dillsburgh, the MP who tried to fly in his car. A sudden thought. A hunch. A possibility. I went back into my bedroom and rang Mary King. She sounded tired and spent.

"Mary, what was Jimmy the Stump's surname?"

"Mullins," she said.

HDJMMK. HD Hugh Dillsburgh. JM Jimmy Mullins. What's in a name? The killer had said. Everything, apparently. It was a hit list. With the realization came another. MK. Mary King. King. A royal goodbye. She was next.

"Mary. Make sure your doors are locked. Close the curtains. Keep away from windows. Make your kids lie on the floor. I'll be there soon."

"OK," she said.

It was as if she was expecting it.

Chapter VII

'Misconceptions play a prominent role in my view of the world.'

George Soros

I drove fast and stupidly. Every driver in front seemed determined to hold me up so I did a lot of swerving and honking and trusting to luck. On CCTV it would not look like an exciting movie car chase but a ridiculous beaten up old Saab driven badly by a ridiculous beaten up old driver. I arrived in Mayes Road, Wood Green and found the nondescript three bedroomed terrace house. Curtains closed. A light in an upstairs room. All quiet.

I texted her to say I was outside. Moments later a curtain opened slightly. Then the door opened and I slipped in. In the shadowy hall she looked pale and lost.

"Where are your kids?"

"Asleep," she said. "What's this about?"

"It's a precaution. The person we're dealing with is unpredictable."

The lie sounded hollow to us both.

"Oh shit. He's going to kill us," she said, and leaned into me.

Her breath smelled of mint toothpaste and fear. We went into her kitchen and I switched on a small desk lamp. I wondered if he'd seen me arrive. Presumably he had. He knew he'd created a little drama of terror and would be nearby enjoying it. I was beginning to hate this psycho, but a part of me was also simply curious, perversely intrigued. What was at the heart of this? I looked at her laptop with the Little Pony sticker. She needed protecting, I would do all I could but I had a sense this had circles within circles. She made instant coffee. While her back was turned I lifted the Little Pony sticker and put a micro tracker underneath. It might come in useful if she went missing. I registered a few details of her life – a calendar with pictures of

Fiji, a gym bag, an ancient wok with the remains of a meal in it, a child's coat.

"Perhaps you should call the police. They can offer you protection that I can't," I said.

She sniffed derisively.

"Police. Do you know how interested they are in the wife of a dead con?" She made a zero with her right index finger and thumb. "And besides, they get so many people threatening others these days I'd be on the C list to check out. They can't act until something actually happens, by which time it's usually too late. No, you may not be Bruce Willis but you're all I've got and all I can afford."

"You must stop flattering me," I said.

She smiled.

"Are you as fucked up as you look?" she asked.

"Much more so. Appearances are deceptive."

"Appearances are all we've got," she said.

This was a good sign. Her life was being threatened, her husband dead, but she was still flirting. I didn't kid myself it was because I looked like a Greek God. It was simply that I was there and

I doubt if she got out much. She went to check on her children. I took a few sips of coffee and then my phone beeped. Text from number unknown: *You Miss the point. G.* More games. Another puzzle. What the hell did this mean? I had something wrong, but what? Hugh Dillsburgh and Jimmy Morrison, both on the list and both dead. MK should be Mary King but I'd missed the point. What point? Did it not mean Mary?

"Did your husband know anyone with the initials MK?" I asked.

She frowned and mentally checked off people.

"Have you got an address book?"

She went and got a book from the hall. I flipped to K and there were two possibilities. Mike Kincardine and Melissa Kinlet.

"Mike's my cousin. Haven't seen him in ten years. Melissa Kinlet's an old school mate. Lives in Australia," she said.

I looked at the message again. A capital M on Miss. Perhaps it wasn't Mary King, but Miss...No, no, no. It couldn't be. Surely it had to be someone connected with Andy King? Surely not Miss Knight. Anna Knight. My Anna. My throat dried.

"I have to go."

Mary's eyes whitened with fear. She held my arm.

"Please. Stay. With me," she said.

She was very scared, but she was also very lonely and needy. Fear does strange things to the body – laughter, desire, all manner of inappropriate demons leap from the dark.

"I'm not Bruce Willis, remember?" I said. "Believe me, I was wrong. You're not in danger, but someone else I know is, and I have to go to them."

She let me go and I slipped out into the night. On the twenty five minute drive I went through every permutation on why it would be pointless to hurt Anna, except I knew that the very futility of it was the point to this man. To show me there were no boundaries, nothing that can't be done, no frontier that wouldn't be crossed in this elaborate game, the purpose of which I was no closer to establishing.

*

She looked so young. Curled foetally, wearing the same white slip as when I'd left earlier in the day. Beautiful brown shoulders with a bloodied swollen necklace of pain where the garrotte had squeezed the life from her. Probably the same garrotte that killed Jimmy. The murderer would like that continuity. Anna's lips salty and bloated blue, her eyes coldly open. She'd been dead maybe three hours. I realised I knew nothing about her family or background, which was how she liked it. I knew her body so well, and her heart not at all. The door had been left unlocked – he knew I'd be coming. I slumped on the floor beside her and held her hand and said goodbye. This was my fault. If my chaos of a life had not led the killer to her she would still be alive, perhaps even sleeping in someone else's arms, dreaming her strange life of ghosts and shadows and unknowns. There were a few bloody hairs under her right index finger. I took two and put them in a small plastic envelope. The police would have no forensic luck in using the hair to find the killer – he was too sharp. Yet perhaps the fact that he hadn't noticed them signified an unwise braggadocio.

Anna had obviously put up a hell of a fight. A lamp and chair overturned, broken glass from photograph frames on the carpet, the TV imploded on the floor. Did no one hear? The phone rang. Without thinking I answered.

"Hello darling. It's Mum."

Oh holy shit.

"I'm sorry, she's not here now," I said and put down the phone.

I stood and looked around. My prints would be all over the flat, all over Anna. Pointless to try and clean everywhere. Perhaps the killer was setting me up and already the police were on their way. Murder, rape. How could they not think me guilty? I would. And in some fundamental sense it was true. I made a feeble attempt at wiping surfaces. I knew the killer would have either worn gloves or wiped all prints from anywhere he touched. He would now be intrigued – how had this affected me? Whatever his prime purpose in these murders was he now had a secondary interest – bettering me at every turn. My only chance of getting near him was to keep calm. Not show my cards, despite the fact I wanted to rip out his throat with my teeth.

I found a key and opened the spare room. I'd never been in there before and she kept it locked. She always joked that the next lover was waiting in there. My heart gagged. It was so entirely unexpected. The room was a clutter of memorabilia, tokens that proclaim a childhood and a life. Photographs of family. School reports. Cheap teenage jewellery. A battered hockey stick. A collection of plastic hairbrushes. A doll with faded golden hair on the pillow. A little arrangement of shells on a shelf forming a letter – P. Paul or perhaps some other ghost or lover from the past she never shared. This was the self she kept carefully hidden. All gone now. I took one of the little shells – a butterfly, put it in my pocket, and left.

I telephoned an ambulance from a public phone, and then went to the university. In my room I could hear Alfred shuffling under the tea towel that some kind soul had placed over his cage. I lifted it off and he blinked sagely. He seemed genuinely surprised to see me.

"*Into the valley of death*," he said.

"How bloody right you are, my friend."

I got a bottle of Famous Grouse from my filing cabinet and switched on the computer. Now I'd stopped the full impact of Anna's death hit me. A young woman dead because she mistakenly took a middle aged wreck for a lover. The killer had had the upper hand all along. Perhaps it was time to realise my limitations and tell the police everything I knew. I hated the thought because I didn't work with the police, didn't trust them and they certainly wouldn't like what I do. Everything pointed to my guilt and why would they bother to look further for Anna's killer? And as Mary said, they would be unlikely to help her. Also, I was angry. I wanted badly to get this man. I needed to win. I decided I would work on this until I dropped. Hard work and whisky were always good antidotes to grief. I texted Cass to say I'd see her tomorrow. Then I texted her again and asked her to reply. Anna's murder had made the world tremble and I needed to know my girl was OK. She texted back: *You're too old for all-nighters xxx*

"If anything happened to Cass the world would end. I love her so much, Alfred, yet I rarely tell her. What kind of fuckwit am I? I'd do anything for her."

Alfred considered this, then head-butted his mirror. He understood me perfectly.

Chapter VIII

'The first Law of nature is that every man ought to endeavour peace, as far as he has hope of obtaining it; and when he cannot obtain it, that he may seek and use all helps and advantages of war.'

Hobbes

I puzzled over the connections between Andy King and Hugh Dillsburgh. A background check on Dillsburgh did little but reveal him as an egotistical and ambitious man with a talent for dirty work. An MP who craved distinction. The jag and the country estate he lived in suggested another source of income as there was no inherited money. I also tried the Rod Whiteley number again and got lucky.

"Who's this?"

"A friend of Andy King."

"Never 'eard of 'im."

"OK. I just had some useful information."

"What are you talkin' about?"

"I can't say on the phone."

He hung up. My phone rang seconds later.

"What's your name?"

"Paul Rook."

"OK Rooky. Five p.m. today. I'll ring you later to tell you where."

At least something was happening. I also decided that, much as I wanted to slowly disembowel him, I would contact David, former friend and present fornicator with the love of my life, Lizzie. A bold decision ably assisted by a quarter bottle of Famous Grouse, grief, guilt, and it was still only 3 a.m. The bastard might be useful with some inside info on Dillsburgh and I formed a vague plan. I phoned his mobile. He sounded groggy.

"David."

"Paul – is that you?"

"Among others. I need to see you."

"It's three bloody a.m."

"I didn't mean now, you imbecile. Tomorrow will do."

"I'm in the house tomorrow."

"Then you'll have a kettle handy to brew some tea. Say three. And if Lizzie is there tell her I love her and I want my Rolling Stones records back, especially *Beggars Banquet*."

I hung up. Anna was dead. Mysterious, nascent, salacious, unknown, secretive, amorphous Anna was dead. Anna the *oeillade*. Anna keeper of secrets. All her chapters unwritten. A surge of grief biled in my throat. I swallowed it with another large whisky, then realised I hadn't eaten since lunchtime yesterday. I found some stale crackers in a file marked EXISTENTIALISM and shared them with Alfred, and then before I keeled over I staggered to the small sofa and my lights went out. In an abysmal chaos of dreams I was hopelessly trying to evade capture by some nameless, shadowy form that appeared in the distance, or on a staircase, or through a window, no matter where I ran or hid. At one point I sat on some concrete steps and wept at the relentlessness of everything, the impossibility of escape or peace.

"Don't hit me, please, don't hit me. I haven't said anything. I don't know anything. Just go away. Please."

I lurched awake to Alfred screeching Jimmy's last words. Tears streamed down my cheeks. My eyes felt like raw onions. It was just before nine. My head was completely fried. The door opened and Mrs. Simpson came in. She went straight to Alfred and gave him a few grapes, then looked at me. She left the room and returned five minutes later with two aspirin and a mug of coffee.

"Dr. Rook, you look like you've had your greens strained backwards through a Scotsman's tights. And it smells like an old tart's jodhpurs in here. It's not fair on Alfred – he's such a finiticky, clean little soul," she said, bustling around annoyingly.

Alfred preened himself and wolf whistled her, which made her giggle like a young girl. I felt like a stranger in my own life, which I was. I closed my eyes and heard her leave. I sipped the coffee and decided the best thing I could do was go home and sleep for a few hours, but the door opened and Cass came in, followed by seven other students. She took in the scene quickly and whispered: "Dad, it's our first seminar on Natural Law. Get yourself together."

There was no way out. They all sat expectantly. I cleared my throat and looked blearily at a young man with close set eyes and an Adam's apple that bobbed like a fishing float. I had no idea of his name.

"Er, Adam…"

"Ben," he corrected.

"Adam, Ben, of course. Can you remind us what, according to Aquinas, are the four kinds of law."

The fishing float bobbed furiously.

"Aquinas distinguishes four main kinds of law: the eternal, the natural, the human, and the divine. Eternal is at the top, then natural, then human. Divine law supposedly reaches human beings by a sort of revelation."

"Good. And how would you define Natural Law?"

"I think it comes from Plato and Aristotle. That nature is good and the natural law that comes from this presupposes that people have a natural tendency towards maintaining good for others. A sort of natural justice."

"That's a big jump – from law to justice."

Adam blushed furiously.

"I just wanted to establish the big picture," he said.

"Very good," I said. "Now I want you all to go away and spend the rest of today writing a short paper entitled: *If Natural Law is innate in all people, why do we need a judicial machine to enforce it?*"

"Do you mean the police and courts and stuff?" asked a spotty boy with an annoying sniff and MP3 wires hanging around his head as if his insect brain had unravelled.

"That's precisely what I mean. Now go away."

They shuffled out mottled with grumbles. Cass remained, looking at me.

"What?" I asked.

"You know what. You can't cancel everything. It's not fair," she said.

"Education is about what you teach yourself," I said pompously. "Besides, I'm starting to realise something. The man I'm after sees himself as a palliative." She suddenly became interested. "Natural Law depends on a view of the world as being ordered. Principles that underlie behaviour. If someone thinks that order has a spanner in the works and chaos reigns then..."

"If they were egotistical enough they might want to put things right. A sort of Natural Law engineer."

"As they see it."

"An avenging angel."

"Pale Rider. Yes. But mostly it's trying to restore order, not dish out punishment."

"Can I help?"

"Sure. You can clean out Alfred's cage," I said, kissing her on the cheek and ambling away, feeling a little less ill. I had a lot to do.

As I left Ron waylaid me. He smiled sheepishly.

"I'm late for a meeting, Ron."

"I was wondering if you'd had any more thoughts," he said.

"I've had lots of thoughts, Ron. None of them about you. You're the sort of person who immediately slips off the radar. Sometimes it's hard to acknowledge you even when you're there."

He smiled. My attempts at escape were failing abysmally.

"You see, that's what I like about you," he said. I looked blank. "Your rudeness. Your indifference to me. It's somehow vital, alive, sort of Lawrentian – all the things I'm not."

Oh God. I had a raving masochist on my hands. There was only one thing to do. I took his chubby cheeks in my hands and gave him a full smacking wet kiss on the lips. It shut him up completely. He stared ahead, his eyes like cold fried eggs. As I walked away I was aware that the Head of Department, the bovine and insipid Audrey Pritchard, had her door open and had seen the whole thing.

Chapter IX

'Live in danger. Build your cities on the slopes of Vesuvius.'

Nietzsche

I went home to shower and change. I was past sleep by now. It would catch up with me tomorrow and I'd be strange and petulant – nothing new there. Symon was slumped in front of the TV watching a tractor pulling competition on a Belgian TV channel. And I thought I was in trouble.

"I didn't realise you were that depressed," I said.

"Just unwinding from a life of toil and stress."

"Rich bastard loafing from where I stand."

"Actually I wasn't watching anyway. I was thinking about your mum. I always liked her."

"I should go and see her," I said, guilt immediately kicking in.

"Let's do it. Now."

"I can't. I've got things to do."

The truth was I had over five hours before meeting with David, so half an hour later we arrived at the small nursing home where my mother spends the days in either a fog or a hallucinogenic carnival, I never knew which. Seeing her was an ordeal, not just because she was so reduced by incipient dementia, but because I was still angry with her for not telling me the name of my father, or giving me some clue that I could pursue. Now it was probably too late – she wouldn't remember even if she wanted to, although her mind came and went. Reason tells me that she was trying to protect me from a man who was on the wrong side of the law. Perhaps she feared I would go to the bad. She didn't understand that there are a thousand ways of doing that, and they don't all involve the law. I've tried several of them.

We sat down in her little room, the TV flickering out some mindless bland daytime trash that she probably never looked at. A lot of fat people with bad teeth were shouting at each other. I unwrapped an Everton mint and gave it to her. She looked at it uncomprehendingly, then there was a flicker of a smile and she took it, popped it in her mouth and started to suck noisily. I never knew from one visit to the next how much of her would still be here, how much there was left to disappear. The colours ran a little drier each time. I followed a routine of telling her that everything was fine – job, marriage, Cass – a little bundle of lies that took about ten minutes, then there was silence, except for the sweet sucking. If she had her teeth in it would end with a few crunches. I love her but we have no common landscape now. The best part of my visit is when I kiss her goodbye and I turn at the door and she gives a little wave. She must have some sort of strange inner life because there is a notepad by her bed, full of scrawled drawings of bizarre phantasms – birdlike creatures and flying stick harpies; perhaps these are her companions in the darkness where her mind has tripped to. The odd thing is that no one ever sees her draw them. They simply appear several times a week.

Come with me, more than forty ragged years ago, to a basement flat in a building held together by soot and bad dreams, to Whitechapel Victorian tenement buildings before the area became sanitised and yuppified by BBC executives. These were playgrounds of ill health, bad sanitation and community feeling punctuated by extreme violence. My mother took a bus west to clean for the well off, then came back to look after me. We had two rooms and a shared toilet and I washed every night at the sink in a closet kitchen. It was Hogarthianly grim, but I knew no better and my imagination was fired by the squalor and the nightly stories my Mum told me about the area. She'd lean back with a cup of tea, old slippers on, still a young woman but ancient to me, and talk about the East End: fragments, ghosts, half remembered anecdotes. Now, I think she was talking to herself mostly and not to a terrified but entranced eight year old: "There was old one-eyed Marty who drank with Fergie the dwarf and they was doing a tailor's shop one night but Marty left the hand brake off the van they was loading on account of his one eye and it rolled down and smacked 'em both into the wall. Only way they could tell which was which when they scraped 'em off is that there was less of Fergie. Stupid takin' a dwarf on a job like that – anyone who clocks 'im will remember. Jack the Ripper did all his business around here. There was others too. Springheel Jack. Killed people then escaped across the rooftops like he had a devil in him. My Aunt Peg swore she saw the ghost of 'im once in Bateman's Row makin' 'is way to Liverpool street where 'e 'id in the sidings. If you saw 'im 'e knew and you was done for."

Such was the literary content of my education. I spent much of my childhood trying not to look up in case I saw Springheel Jack and his red eye torched me and I would be marked for a grisly butcher's death. Something of all this settled in my soul and is still broiling there, and makes me watchful, suspicious, intoxicated with the night. Even as a minnow I realised I was in the grip of something because as much as I fearfully watched the rooftops for the shadow, the switchblade eye, the quick jump and slice in the dark, I also started to crave it. I wanted to see him and, more importantly, to be seen, to register in the consciousness of the downright wicked. The prickle on the back of my neck became a strange friend. It is like the kick people get from slash fest and horror movies, only I wanted it real. I liked the taste of fear, the cordite of danger in my nostrils, the quickening rush through the brain. That's when it started for me. A psychologist would say that was the moment my pathological obsession activated; I would say that was when the great adventure started, half in love with easeful death, as Keats would have it. The killer I was seeking now had something of this shadowy childhood world about him. My mum did her best and I love her for it. I just wish she'd given me a name to follow.

*

Symon smiled, moved his chair closer and took her hand. He started humming, then singing softly 'Summertime' from Porgy and Bess. He sang in a husky baritone and looked directly into her eyes.

Slowly she focussed and returned the look. When he got to the refrain 'So hush little baby, don't you cry' she joined in, a birdlike croaky warble that broke my heart. She closed her eyes on the end note and when she opened them she smiled warmly at him, then at me.

"Symon," she said. "Nice lad. Full of mischief, but you can't 'elp liking 'im."

My hangover blistered and fell apart. I grabbed her bony little hands in mine.

"That's right, Mum. That's right. My friend Symon. He came round after school."

"Cupcakes," she said, then her eyes flickered and she eclipsed, her hands dropped and she stared expressionlessly at the floor.

"Remember?" said Symon.

Of course I did. As a special treat on a Friday she'd bring in two cupcakes for us, with a glass of milk. We felt like princes. Symon had opened a door. We stayed a few more minutes, I kissed her goodbye, she waved at me, then we left.

"I'm grateful," I said as we drove back to my flat.

"We're friends."

"When we were young did she ever say anything about my father?" I asked.

He took his time.

"Sorry, Paul. Nothing. But if you want help in tracing him…"

"It's OK. I've tried every route I can think of. It's a stupid obsession."

I decided to break a habit. It was a risk but everything important is precisely that. I took a deep breath and told him about my other life, and my interest in the shadowy side of humanity. As he listened I was reminded of what I liked about Symon – he never judged. He listened and weighed up and responded, but you never had to feel guarded. I even told him about Anna. When I'd finished he took his time, digesting all this new and improbable information about me.

"Jesus. You could always surprise me. There I was thinking you'd settled for backwater academia. I don't know what to say. But you have to be careful, Paul. Whoever this nutter is, he's a minefield."

I nodded. The one thing I didn't tell him is that I liked the danger; it was a form of addiction. More than that, I felt seduced by it.

"I was wondering if you'd help," I asked.

He looked surprised.

"You have a map in your head of how international business works. I'm trying to trace a company – Ocean Investment. It's not registered but it made payments to Andy King. I have box numbers but nothing else."

"I'll get on it, I need something to do," said Symon. "*Il est nécessaire de travailler, sinon par goût, au moins par désespoir.*"

"'It is necessary to work, if not from inclination, at least from despair.' Baudelaire." I said. "I forgot how much you liked him. You always were a miserable sod."

"You and me together. He's the only thing I can remember from University. My head's been full of excel spread sheets, export contracts and profit margins for the past fifteen years. Actually, helping you out will be a breath of fresh air."

Chapter X

'I won't slave for beggar's pay
likewise gold and jewels
but I would slave to learn the way
to sink your ship of fools'
Robert Hunter

I walked past Parliament and towards Portcullis House, where a lot of MPs, including bastard David, had offices. The whole world and its dog seemed to be taking photographs of other people taking photographs. It baffled me that Parliament had become a tourist theme park when the only person who should be allowed near it is Guy Fawkes. Portcullis House is a suitably ambiguous name, with associations of fortification, I guess mostly to keep dirty little secrets in and questions out. It was designed to resemble and feel like a ship inside, with offices and passages of bowed windows and light oak finishing. Presumably the metaphor is meant to suggest a wise ship of state, steering the nation to calmer waters and greater prosperity. I think a ship of fools all at sea in an impending storm with no one among the crazed cargo of deluded fools aboard able to read a compass accurately is more appropriate. The fact that it is not really a ship is a good allegory for all governments – they do not really govern and are simply there to create the illusion that we have choice. The world is actually run by a cartel of mega rich people who have most of the money, own the resources, take the profits, run the banks, and own or influence the media so we only know what we are allowed to know, and most of that is a dung heap of lies. Some call this conspiracy thinking – I call it reality.

Such were my happy thoughts as I was frisked for the third time by an apparatchik armed with a pistol and a pepper spray, questioned by a young woman smiling like a predatory snake, and photographed by at least three dozen CCTV cameras. This Stalinist welcome combined with my hangover and the emotional scene with my mother created a lethal brew of rage and despair, and I had to take a few deep breaths to refrain from punching David in the face as he approached, smiling blandly and wearing an Armani suit paid for out of the public purse. I could see he was deliberating on whether or not to hold out a welcoming hand – rejection would make him look foolish, but not to do so might seem overtly frosty. I realised that he probably gauged every move like that now – not in terms of its value but how it would be perceived. Life as a giant PR manoeuvre. I put my hands firmly in my pockets to settle the matter for him.

"Paul. Let me sign you in," he said.

I signed various bits of paper and was issued with a little badge, and then he led me into the bowels of the building. He was nervous, but also curious. He hoped that I was there to say that we could now all be grown up about things and the fact that he was bedding my wife was fine. Unless he had become a complete moron he'd also know that wasn't going to happen. Finally we entered a small, clean office and I sat on a cheap IKEA chair while he sat on a £400 upholstered, swivel desk chair.

"I'm glad you phoned. It's time we cleared the air."

I decided to let him take the lead.

"I suppose it's because Lizzie has told you," he continued.

I smiled.

"That I've asked her to marry me."

"Of course," I lied. This was a bombshell.

"All I ask, Paul, for the sake of our…of what was our friendship…is that you respect the fact that I do genuinely love her and agree to a divorce. ASAP. Let's be civilised about it."

I furrowed my brow and nodded sagely, revealing nothing of the seething cocktail of bile I was now becoming. My organs burned. His computer was on, which was what I'd hoped. My hangover was another piece of luck, as I looked like a corpse.

"Are you alright? You look terrible, I mean, you always look terrible, but you look even worse," he said.

"Actually I don't feel too well. You haven't got an aspirin, have you?" I said.

"Got some paracetamol somewhere," he said, looking through a drawer.

"No, I react badly to them. You haven't got aspirin?"

"Hang on. I'll see if anyone in the café has any," he said, and like a fool left the room. At worst I was hoping to prise Hugh Dillsburgh into the conversation, but this was better. I took the USB stick from my pocket and started to download all his emails. Then I had a quick look through the files and downloaded one called PRESS ISSUES. I finished with about three seconds to spare before David returned. He gave me a couple of aspirin and I swallowed one with a gulp of Commons spring water.

"Paul, I know this has all been a bit of a mess, and I'm truly sorry. What do you think?" he asked.

"About it being a mess, about you being sorry, about being civilised, or what?"

"You know what. A divorce."

I'd got more than I'd hoped for, so I didn't have to pretend any more.

"I think the only reason you want to marry Lizzie is because you're worried about your public image, because you're a pathetically ambitious little snot who wants a nice respectable marriage to help brownnose your slimy way up the career ladder, and it has nothing to do with love or desire or hunger or anything I could understand, or even, God forbid, respect.."

His eyes narrowed and his lips thinned.

"You come into my place of work, into bloody parliament, just to insult me?" he said, his cheeks whitening.

"Where would you rather I go?" I asked.

"Paul, you're an insecure, egotistical shit," he said.

"Well done. Something real at last."

"Get out."

"You're a parasite, David, even to the extent that you want to feed on the smoking ruin of my marriage. You're a flaccid, self-entranced little grub squatting your furry arse along with all the other little grubs in this factory of lies and incompetence, all hoping to steal from the public purse. I hope a drone missile cops the lot of you one day soon and that I'm here to watch it." Absolutely childish stuff, but great fun.

He called Security on an internal phone and moments later a guard tooled up with enough weapons to fell a herd of buffalo appeared and smiled.

"Get him out," David said.

"Would you come with me, sir?"

"Are you asking me on a date?" I said.

"I like a comedian. You can tell me a joke on the way out."

He was surprisingly strong and a few minutes later I found myself on the pavement. I was feeling better already. The whiff of risk and danger had warmed my blood. I went to a café and looked at the USB on my laptop. A lot of soap opera emails about who said what or who might vote which way. I would read them all more carefully later. A few from Lizzie: *You're the only one...your integrity, openness, the opposite of Paul...I love the smell of you, your hands on my back...*And there it was – an email about Hugh Dillsburgh with the phrase: *It really does look like a heart attack.* Why the word 'really'? This suggested there might be another reason for his death. Then six emails mentioning Ocean Investment. One was very telling: *We cannot prove any links with the government, and in any case considering it was our baby we'd be in murky waters.* This from Henry Kellas, a player in their ever burgeoning team of Press Officers. I looked in the PRESS ISSUES file. Several things interested me, but I only looked at one on OCEAN INVESTMENT. A lot of boring data but one telling phrase: *The weapons link must not get out, esp. re D.*

Now I had something. I didn't have a clue what exactly, but when the fog cleared then perhaps faces, names and events would appear. Whatever all this was it seemed that both Government and Opposition were in bed together over it. It also gave me something to use with the mysterious Rod Whiteley. I'd been texted and told where to go – the café in Dulwich Park. I just had time to get there. As I stood I got a text: *Natural Law is preferable to political deceptions. You should know that by now. Remember the First Law of Nature. Gladiator.* Number unknown. He was still watching me. I looked around, suspecting everyone and everything. The first Law of nature is from Hobbes' Leviathan: '*...that every man ought to endeavour peace, as far as he has hope of obtaining it; and when he cannot obtain it, that he may seek and use all helps and advantages of war*'. This character was at war with everyone, perhaps even me. I wondered if by going to see Rod Whiteley, whoever he was, I was putting him in trouble too.

Chapter XI

'Everything in this world sweats crime: the newspaper, the wall, the face of mankind.'
Baudelaire

I sat in the Dulwich Park café sipping a coffee. Ten minutes after five another text told me to go to the Crown and Greyhound and wait in the first bar on the left facing the pub. The pub is also known as the Dog, a big listed building, a fusion of two Victorian pubs, with an impressive fresco front. I ordered a Famous Grouse and sat by the door. A tall, forty-something, athletic-looking man in a leather jacket, far more expensive than my battered relic, was reading a paper opposite me. I knew he was aware of me and he eventually got up and as he passed me, said without looking, "Outside now. Silver Audi."

A driver stared straight ahead and a tubby man with bulldog jowls and Father Christmas eyes sat in the back. I got in next to him and the man from the pub slammed the door, and then joined the driver in the front. The car eased away and I waited for what was next.

"Are you Rod Whiteley?" I asked.

"Shut up," said tubby man. I never did like Father Christmas.

He took a blindfold from his pocket and indicated that I was to wear it.

"I suffer panic attacks in the dark," I said.

"Make it a quiet attack then," he said, and tied it securely around my head. We drove for about twenty minutes, and then the car stopped. I was helped out, and led along a path. A door opened and I was ushered through. In the bizarre landscape I inhabit I was almost enjoying this intrigue, the helplessness of being led. Where would it lead? When you cannot see your mind ignites; I imagined a Gothic castle with torches, hunchback servants and Jacobean secrets. Will I never grow up?

"Steps," someone said.

An arm guided me up and then stopped me and a door was opened. I was led through, and continued to walk. We turned left, another door opened, and I was halted. The acoustics were strange, slightly echoing.

"You can take it off now," someone said, with a voice like razor blades. A door closed.

I took off the blindfold and blinked in the light. I was in a huge bathroom – mock gold gilded taps in the shapes of dolphins, a swirl bath, dozens of coloured bottles of lotions and shampoos, ornate mirrors that made the place look twice as big. At the far end in a separate little cubicle a man sat on a toilet, his trousers ballooned around his ankles and shirttails hanging over the sides of the toilet seat like modesty curtains. He'd been reading the *Daily Mail* but now held it, scrutinising me. He looked miserable and discombobulated. A little table was next to the toilet, home to a coffee pot and two cups.

"Coffee?" he asked.

"No thanks."

He poured for himself.

"You're wondering, so I'll tell you. Irritable bowel syndrome. Chronic. Wouldn't recommend it. Irregular motions. Excessive flatulence. Urgent calls of nature. Never know what's coming next. So I take what you might call extreme precautionary measures. Most of my working day is in here, except when I'm in the field."

"The field?"

"Just an expression. Life's a battle, especially if you got bowels like mine. Where dogs have IBS, suspected causal factors are thought to be related to diet intolerances, possibly allergies, the inability of food to effectively pass through the gastrointestinal tract, and mental distress. Suspect the same may be true of humans. With ferrets, a sure sign of the disease is lethargy, and a lethargic ferret – not a pretty sight, especially if you're a handler. Ball's in your court, Mister Rook."

"I was hoping you might be able to help me. Andy King."

"Your message was singularly explicit. You said you had information to impart. Useful information at that. Now you're asking for fucking help. That is a completely different barrel of eels."

He broke wind loudly and musically.

"See what you've done now. All hell could break loose down there. And on your head be it. I can feel fructose malabsorption or even gastroesophageal reflux coming on lively, and if that is the case, the space you occupy in the world is soon to become vacant."

I wondered if the mention of Andy had brought on this onslaught of wind and hostility.

"Mister Whiteley, I actually came here to warn you, to help. Trying to gain information was a secondary purpose. I'm a friend of the King family. We go way back, so when Andy was murdered I tried to help Mary and the kids. I know you had some business dealings with Andy, and I think a company called Ocean Investment might have been involved in his death. I simply came to say be careful, but I didn't realise you were such an eminent man, with your own people. I'm sorry if I wasted your time."

He digested this, but not much else to judge by the growls and rumblings he was producing. It wasn't so much a body he inhabited as a chemical factory.

"Andy was out of his league and a liability. It was only a matter of time."

He hadn't asked about Ocean Investment, which suggested he knew the company.

"I'm worried that whatever Andy was into, it might affect Mary and the kids. Is there anything I can say to her that will help?"

"You can tell her to marry someone with a brain next time around."

"What was it he was doing that was so dangerous?"

His eyes narrowed and his bowels quietened.

"Why do you want to know?"

"I was his friend. Since we were kids."

"What school did he go to?"

"Lambeth. Lambeth High."

"I'm going to let you go now, Mister Rook, but only for the sake of my bowels. They've had enough of a stir for one day. You are dismissed. And it was fucking Broadway Road School. Lambeth my arse. Buy a lottery ticket. This is your lucky day. If I was in a better mood I'd have had you hospitalised."

The leather jacket man entered as if on cue, put a blindfold on me and I was led out. He drove me back in silence to the Crown and Greyhound and he took off the blindfold. I went inside and ordered a Famous Grouse. A text: *Another escape. Lucky boy. Gladiator.* Number unknown. I looked and saw the leather coat man still in the Audi outside. He was looking down. I stood and saw that he was holding a phone. He turned and looked straight at me. I walked outside towards the car. Was this the bastard who had killed Anna and was playing games with me? He smiled and drove away. Had I found my Nemesis? If so I needed a name.

Chapter XII

'The natural law of inertia: Matter will remain at rest or continue in uniform motion in the same straight line unless acted upon by some external force.'

W. Clement Stone

"It's not a lot, but it's something."

Symon spread out his notes on the coffee table. He seemed more animated than usual, obviously enjoying his soiree into the underworld. He had discovered via various business acquaintances that Ocean Investment was involved in trading currencies, but had a reputation for insider dealing and skirting the fringes of the law, but as he said, that's what most legitimate businesses do, including banks, and they just have the law changed if they don't like it. He said he'd carry on enquiring. He was also intrigued that I had found my stalker – a mystery man who worked for, or with, Rod Whiteley. I said I felt I had too little information on Andy King – who he was, what his role actually was. I didn't have him clear in my mind.

"Try being him," said Symon. "Think John Locke. There's a continuity of consciousness, a process of thoughts that are predictable and make up Andy King." Clearly Symon had remembered nuggets from his philosophy degree, despite what he'd said.

I smiled. "OK. I'm thirty eight. Beautiful wife…"

"Stop there. How does she make you feel?"

"Love her. She's vulnerable, sexy, clever. More clever than me."

"Does that make you feel threatened?"

"Makes me feel I have to prove myself."

"So when you got this offer?"

"Dream deal. More money than I usually get. Respect."

"And you wanted people to know. Andy King is on his way. Big player."

"Yes. But that was also a mistake."

"Right. Make public what has to be kept secret and you're in the mire."

"Exactly. I'm putting myself, and my family, in danger. Stupid."

"Your own worst enemy."

"That's me."

"You had it coming."

"No. I didn't."

"Who killed you?"

"Bloke I knew."

"Someone you worked with?"

"Yes. I think so. He considered me a risk."

We took this process for a longer walk until I had a stronger sense of who Andy King might have been. It was a great help and Symon was good at asking searching questions. Perhaps after a lifetime of secrecy and working in the shadows, I'd found a working partner. As students we'd been philosophy soul mates. Perhaps we could be again. Perhaps life was going to change significantly. Anna's murder made it even more imperative that I find this killer.

We now suspected that Andy had been involved in illegal currency trading, as was Rod Whiteley, and that a man I'd just met who worked for or with Rod could be the psychotic serial killer, a man of delitescent powers who was killing off people who might give me information. I needed to know exactly what Andy's role was. Clearly he was no financial wizard, so there must have been some aspect of the trading that involved physical carriage and risk taking. I pondered all this as I drove to the university. I suspected I was going to have to visit Prague before long. I decided that I would invent a conference and invite myself as speaker so that the university would pay my expenses. It would also make Audrey Pritchard think I'm actually doing something.

*

Alfred had settled in well. He was much more popular than I was, which wasn't difficult. I let him out of his cage and he flew around the room and settled on my shoulder and nibbled my ear. He was a perfect mimic and treated me to a few choice remarks. Mrs Simpson's "Luvverly cuppa, darlin'," the Security Guard's "Ello feathers, 'ows it 'anging?" and my own pompous pontifications: "Hume said: 'man is a bundle or collection of different perceptions which succeed one another with an inconceivable rapidity and are in perpetual flux and movement', so this complicates questions of innocence, guilt and moral culpability." It made me realise what a prize pillock I often am.

I had a seminar in which the students discussed their papers on Natural Law. They trooped in and took seats.

"We need a justice system because although people may have, as a Platonic principle, an innate sense of justice, they may choose not to act on it. So free will complicates any ability people have to know right from wrong," said the boy with the bobbing Adam's apple.

"But who's to say everyone has the same innate sense of natural law? What I think is just or unjust may be different to what you think. That's why we need certain agreed broad principles which the state can enforce," said a girl with a barbed wire necklace tattooed around her throat.

"But what happens if someone decides that only they are qualified to mete out justice, perhaps even execution?" asked Cass, looking at me.

"Then they are seriously psycho," said bobbing boy.

If only he knew how right he was. I explained a pet theory of mine, that the ubiquitous sense of justice that children seem to have, the constant cry of "It's not fair," may suggest that there is somewhere in the human psyche a sense of natural justice, and that at some primal archetypal level we all have an internal judge and occasional executioner who, if life permitted, would mete out justice, retribution and punishment. I sensed that this rang true for all the students except bobble hat. Sometimes I teach well despite myself. It was also territory coming tellingly close to the killer I was hunting.

"*Into the valley of death...*" said Alfred, which seemed a suitable place to stop.

I left Cass in my office to feed Alfred and work on her essay, which is a blessing, given what happened. Half way home I was aware I was being followed by a red Renault. I slowed down and it slowed with me. I almost decided to stop to see what it would do, but thought I would find out just how determined the driver was. I drove around aimlessly for twenty minutes, and then took a narrow country side road. I knew it led to a village, and my plan was to stop at the police station and then sit it out in a game of attrition, but on the next bend I just had time to brake before slamming into the silver Audi. The red Renault nestled behind me. What now?

The tall man in the leather jacket got out of the Audi and approached. He opened my door.

"Shove over," he said.

I moved over. He eased into the driver's seat, moved it back an inch or so to accommodate his long legs, and tried the pedals.

"Shit car," he said, and followed the Audi.

Light chat clearly wasn't his forte. I waited a few minutes. All I could do was see what happened next. Was I really sitting next to Anna's killer? God knows how many others he'd dispatched, as well as Jimmy and Andy King.

"I'm not being blindfolded this time?" I asked.

"No need," he said. "It's a one way trip. Give me your phone."

I gave him my phone. I didn't like the sound of this.

"Who are you?" I asked.

No response.

"You didn't have to kill her," I said. "I thought you were exceptionally clever up until then. But Anna's death was pointless. Why? Just to show you could? Because you thought she might know something about whatever it is they're all involved in?"

He looked ahead. I was trying to bait him to see if he was the killer. Was he this impassive when he killed Andy King, Jimmy, Anna? Maybe this is also how death comes. The drive home, an unexpected turn, a stranger with a twist of madness. I experienced a sudden rush, which I knew to be adrenalin pulsing. I smiled and savoured the feeling while it lasted and before a different kind of fear came visiting. Leather Jacket looked at me as if I needed straitjacketing. Our little wagon train drove for another half an hour, into an industrial area just outside Watford where all industry has stopped – gone bankrupt or in debt or just too tired to produce anything in an England gone to seed. It was depressing. Down a cul-de-sac and eventually we stopped at a nondescript office building with a 'For Sale' sign outside.

"A dream come true. An abandoned business on the outskirts of Watford. Thank you, driver," I said.

He suddenly turned to me, his face full of unknown fury.

"All my life I've wanted to have a clever twat like you this close to pop. And when it comes to it you will shit yourself. Like everyone else I've done. Including bloody Anna. She was begging for it.

Couldn't wait for her lights to be switched off. It was an act of mercy blowing her away."

I was ushered out, through a door and up some stairs. I recognised from the angle and the sounds, and the swish of the door that this was where I had been taken to meet Rod Whiteley. What had happened? The killer in the leather jacket switched on the light and there was Rod, seated in all his trouser-less glory on the toilet seat, but dead, his eyes popped open, his face blue-grey as drain water, his lips a pair of purple slugs. He'd wet himself and his bowels had clearly finally opened altogether to judge by the stench. The small tubby Father Christmas man looked at me.

"OK Mister Not-long-for-this-life, talk. What were you after?"

"The king is dead. Long live the king," I said.

"What?" said Father Christmas.

"Died on the toilet, like Elvis."

He slapped me around the face very hard. It stung like billyo and a ring he wore carved a little blood trail. I could feel the skin split. I tried to compute what was happening. I looked at Leather Jacket.

"You killed him. Now you're setting me up."

He laughed. Father Christmas looked at Leather Jacket for a moment, but then dismissed the thought. Criminals are ever suspicious of each other, even, and sometimes especially, their best friends.

"You came here on some pretext about Andy King, so you'd know where Rod was. It was a set up so you could come back and kill him. It has to be you. Why?" asked Father Christmas.

"That's ludicrous. I had a blindfold on. I didn't know where I was. And what reason could I have for killing him?" I said.

"That's what we want to know. That's why you're here."

"Let me take him outside. If he's got anything to say, believe me, he'll say it," said Leather Jacket.

A minute later I was in a tiny courtyard with a few wheelie bins and Leather Jacket pointed a gun at my head. A rush of adrenalin made me feel electrically alive. I realised I'd got this horribly wrong. He said he'd blown Anna away, but she had been garrotted. Did I miss something? Had she been shot too? No, he'd been lying, just to shut me up.

Chapter XIII

'Philosophy: A route of many roads leading from nowhere to nothing.'

Ambrose Bierce

Nothing made sense. He pushed the gun into my forehead. I could see the wheels in his head cranking infinitesimally towards the absolute and final thrill of pulling the trigger, just for the hell of doing it and hang the reason.

"OK. Why'd you kill Rod? You're a dead man anyway but if you talk I'll do it quick. If not I'll kill you in pieces and you'll be begging me to finish it. Why'd you strangle him?"

"I didn't."

Hurdy-gurdy thoughts Catherine-wheeled around my head as I tried to work out what was happening. Nothing sensible presented itself so I opted for further confusion. Strange how being so close to death creates either trembling terror and paralysis or clarity of sorts. I had a pathetic notion I could seduce this moron with words.

"Presumably you're covering your own tracks by blaming me for Rod's murder. And you still think you're performing some sort of righteous executioner role for God knows what. A dark angel of Natural Law, but let me tell you some scholars take natural law, *lex naturalis*, to be synonymous with natural justice or natural right, so if you assume a symbiotic relationship between law and rights it means that I have a natural right not be treated merely as a punitive object in your singular crusade, but as a parallel agent of justice, despite the fact that you have the gun. I suggest we adjourn this meeting until you have acquainted yourself with the philosophies of Hobbes, Aquinas, Grotius, Locke, and possibly Burlamaqui and Emmerich de Vattel, then we can have an informed…"

I would have continued but he kneed me in the groin and it took my breath away.

"Weirdo," he said.

All this was wrong. This imbecile thug couldn't have sent me the texts or covered his tracks so assiduously. I had to play for time.

"Alright, maybe not Locke. He can be a bit dry, but you might find Samuel von Pufendorf illuminating," I gasped, my groin throbbing horribly.

"Fuck it, I'm just gonna pop you. Rod's dead anyway, so..."

A phone beeped. It was mine. Leather Jacket took my phone from his pocket and looked at it. He smirked and showed it to me. A text: *A man living irrationally has no rational rights. Gladiator.*

"What the fuck sort of message is that?" he asked.

"It's a classic and deeply flawed argument used to justify execution," I said.

"Who the fuck's Gladiator? Is this some sort of queer thing?"

"I have no idea who is sending these messages," I said.

"It's your bloody phone, you nonce," he said.

A beep indicated another text, which we both read: *Rook is now going to take the gun from you and shoot you in your stupid head.* Leather Jacket looked perplexed, then he turned to see who might be watching and that gave me a moment. I kicked him as hard as I could in his left shin. He howled and fell off balance. I grabbed his arm that held the gun with one hand and tried to pull the gun away with the other. He was too strong and held on to it. I kicked him again in the shin and he howled and went down on one knee. I still held the hand with the gun but he grabbed it with his free hand so that each of us had both hands on it and he started twisting it round so that he could shoot me. We circled and gyrated as if involved in some macabre dance.

His breath was stale and oniony. I was no match for his strength. I smashed my own face into his and bit as hard as I could. He twisted away and his upper eyelid flapped open and started spouting blood. I spat out skin and something else and kicked again. This time I caught him squarely in the groin. He wheezed and went down on both knees.

We were still holding the gun with both our hands. I leaned down and bit hard into his left hand. He let go and I snatched the gun away, falling over with the momentum. I got to my feet and faced him. He was still on his knees, his eye a bloody mess. He blinked furiously and spat at me. It had all happened in ten seconds but I was breathing heavily and my legs felt like stone.

My phone was on the floor at my feet. It beeped and vibrated again. I could read the text: *Now finish him*. I pointed the gun at his head. I only had to pull the trigger and this lowlife would be dispatched. I was almost detachedly aware of adrenalin and blood pumping cartwheels around my head.

Then the rush stopped and I was me again, suddenly deflated. Most importantly I was aware I was being played. Merely a puppet in someone else's opera. Everything changed. Leather Jacket sensed it and slowly, in a series of wobbles, got to his feet. He looked at me contemptuously with his unbloodied eye, and smiled. I noticed he had a gold filling in a left incisor.

"Don't have the bottle, do you? You didn't kill Rod. Couldn't have, worm like you. And now I'm going to show you how to do it."

He stepped towards me, and then he suddenly stopped as if an idea as powerful as a bullet had just entered his brain. In fact that is precisely what happened. A perfect hole in his forehead, and he fell backwards like a toppled log and the wound began gushing more blood than I thought a head could hold. His left leg twitched uncontrollably and a stain spread from his crotch where he had wet himself. A mix of foam and mucus dribbled from his mouth. Death is never like the movies. It is often ugly and visceral. Only I hadn't killed him. I looked around, wondering if I was next.

Another text: *Get out now. They'll be coming in a few minutes. Gladiator.* The courtyard had four high walls. Whoever fired the shot must have been on the roof. How did he know I'd be taken here? Was this a strange brew of luck and intelligence? Then I saw a window halfway up a wall – the angle meant the shot had been fired from there. I had to get out before Father Christmas and his cohorts realised something was wrong, but I was also curious. Hell, I'd just escaped death – it wasn't my day to go.

I ran inside and up some stairs, through a few doors and found the room with the window. No one there, of course. I went to a room on the opposite side of a corridor, just in time to look through a window and see a black BMW driving away. An arm raised out of the window gave me a wave. He was wearing a blue bomber jacket. Cheeky. Ridiculous. There was no chance of seeing anything in detail and I only caught an 'M' and an 'R' on the license plate before the car swung round a corner and was gone. I needed to be gone too and ran out of the building. My spare keys were under the driver's seat, and my hand scraped against something else, stuck to the underside. I pulled it off. A small black box, the size of a matchbox. A tracking device; these were something I knew about and I often used them myself, but I preferred small ones, easily hidden. How many others were there, and where were they? And why did he save me? If he'd simply let Leather Jacket kill me then I'd be off his back. As I'd realised before, he now saw us as a team, and if I had shot Leather Jacket as instructed, that would deepen our bond. I suspected it was also something to do with a weird code of honour brewed in the highly coloured crucible of his imagination. Or perhaps I was useful in some other way? There were some people about whom you had to think sideways to track. I drove away as fast as my old Saab would allow.

*

Cass was in my office looking moody and squaring for a fight. I was feeling distinctly wobbly now the adrenalin had worn off. She took in my appearance. My cheek was still bleeding.

"What happened?" she asked.

"I cut myself shaving."

"I've been here hours. Everyone else has gone. You were meant to be here for tutorials."

"I got caught up."

"Caught up with everything except me. You're not even letting me in on the case. And I need to talk."

"When women say that men usually run away," I said.

"Pathetic," she said and left, slamming the door.

"I'm sorry, Cass."

I went out to the corridor but she'd gone. Another moment appallingly handled. I have such a talent for it. Alfred was in a thoughtful mood. I gave him some cobnuts, which he cracked open and ate, eyeing me askance, his eyes like black pearls. He walked along my desk, and then knocked a pile of essays to the floor with his beak.

"Good work, Alfred," I said.

"*Into the valley of death,*" he said contemptuously.

"Exactly," I said. "But how can I be so stupid with my own daughter? When I love her so much."

"*Cannon to the left of them, cannon to the right of them,*" he said.

I knew that, cannon everywhere at the moment, and knowing it wasn't helpful. The door opened and Audrey entered. She seemed to be wearing a giant puce lampshade and earrings like melting globules of mucus. She looked at my cheek.

"It's polite to knock," I said.

"I think you and I know each other well enough to dispense with formalities," she said.

"On the contrary, Professor, our knowledge of each other, professionally, personally and certainly biblically, is so scant as to be non-existent."

"Have you been in a fight?" she asked.

"I'm always in a fight."

"Where were you this afternoon, Dr Rook?"

"I went to see a man who was garrotted on his own toilet, then had an altercation with a gangster who held a revolver to my head, right here…" I pointed to the spot. "…but I was saved by a psychopathic serial killer. And how has your afternoon been?"

"Always sarcastic. I'll cut to it. Your behaviour is unprofessional and unacceptable. You are hardly here. You constantly cancel things. Take this as a formal reprimand. If things don't change soon I'll implement a disciplinary enquiry. And that parrot breaks at least six regulations. Get rid of it."

Alfred shrieked and flew onto the top of my PC.

"Don't hit me, please, don't hit me. I haven't said anything. I don't know anything. Just go away. Please," he shrieked.

Audrey bristled in her lampshade. I tried to imagine her naked and shuddered inwardly at the thought. It would be like looking at skewered tripe.

"That parrot must be out of here by the end of the week."

She left in what she imagined was an authoritative flourish. Alfred and I looked at each other.

"She means it," I said.

"Aquinas distinguishes four main kinds of law: the eternal, the natural, the human, and the divine. Eternal is at the top, then natural, then human. Divine law supposedly reaches human beings by a sort of revelation." Alfred was repeating what had been said during the tutorial. And now an idea started to form in my mind. Ten minutes later it had a definite shape.

I fell asleep on the battered couch as the adrenalin drained and left me exhausted. When I awoke it was dark. I gave Alfred fresh water and left. I was deadbeat and when I saw Ron running towards me down a corridor I scooted and just made it to my car in time. I was looking forward to a hot bath, a large scotch and ten hours sleep. When I got to the flat I went to the kitchen to get my Famous Grouse, opened the door and surprised them, Cass in her dressing gown in Symon's arms, their faces an inch apart. I felt sick. Dizzy. Murderous.

Chapter XIV

'Mysteries are due to secrecy.'
Francis Bacon

Symon looked at me guiltily.

"It isn't what you think, Paul," he said. His arms fell away from Cass.

"As if you know what I think. As if you dare to presume anything about me," I said, squaring up to him.

"Dad! What are you doing? Don't be stupid."

"Stupidity is my forte, Cass. How long has this been going on?"

The anger was bubbling and needed to go somewhere. I kicked over the rubbish bin and noticed there were three empty scotch bottles in it. I really must watch my drinking.

"Paul, if you just let me explain," said Symon.

"All you need to do is pack your grubby things and get out of my flat. You've got five minutes. After that I burn anything left."

I poured a scotch and waited, seething. A few minutes later Symon walked by with his case. He didn't slam the door as he left. Cass looked at me. She was nineteen. A young woman. Did I still want her to be my little girl? My baby? She folded her arms defiantly and looked at me. Suddenly her eyes filled and my heart ached. I went to her.

"Cass, he's my age. What were you thinking?"

She fought back the tears and looked at me.

"He's funny. He listens to me. And I fell in love with him. A bit. That's why I wanted to talk to you, but you were so scratchy. I came back and told him and he said he was your friend and he was too old for me anyway. And now you've embarrassed me and made a complete prat of yourself."

"Why can't you be normal and go for boys your own age?"

She looked at me, genuinely surprised.

"Normal? You dare to ask why I'm not normal. I give up."

She went to her room and slammed the door. She had a point. A father with a double life, a broken marriage, a job he rarely goes to and seemed determined to lose, more a shadow than a human being, full of strange addictions….the list started to depress me so I stopped it. Another scotch was called for. A night of serious thinking and drinking beckoned. Something had been nagging at me. I needed to know. I phoned Symon on his mobile.

"You're a complete bastard and I'm going to castrate you but I need to know something."

"I can hardly wait," said Symon, obviously full of righteous indignation.

"You said Ocean Investment dealt in currencies, but I've got a file that suggests that it deals in weapons, I guess illegally."

"Where did you get that?" he said.

"A private folder belonging to an MP."

"Did it mention names?"

"HD. Perhaps Hugh Dillsburgh."

"Could be. The weapons link surprises me, but it may be that they spread their activities and investments and their link is indirect. Can I say something about Cass?"

"No," I said and ended the call.

I'd overreacted. Symon clearly had tried to extricate himself in a gentlemanly fashion, but the damage was done and I'd have to let Cass cool off. I underestimated her ability to bear a grudge. Now where could she have inherited that from, I wonder?

I sat in the lounge with my laptop and made a list of what I had so far:

WEAPONS LINK: OCEAN INVESTMENT, ANDY KING, HUGH DILLSBURGH, PRAGUE, ROD WHITELEY

This was big enough for at least one political party to be worried. Big enough for five people to be murdered. The body count was alarming. I rang Lizzie.

"It's me," I said.

"Is Cass alright?"

"She's fine. Listen, this is difficult but something's happened and I don't like it. Leaves a bad taste."

"What?"

"I saw David."

"I know. It took two bottles of Chablis to calm him down."

"But that's a girl's drink."

"Paul – is there a point to this?"

"Well, we had a few drinks and he started saying how much he loved you, and you him…and then…"

"Then what?"

"He showed me emails you'd sent him. To prove a point, I suppose. Some sort of competitive drive, to show you love him more than you ever did me. It's childish but made me feel a bit grubby."

"You are grubby. And you're lying."

I quoted verbatim.

"You're the only one…your integrity, openness, the opposite of Paul…I love the smell of you, your hands on my back…"

She put down the phone. I calculated it would take fifteen minutes. Antebellum. Twelve minutes later my phone rang. It was David. I knew he wouldn't have the balls to actually come round.

"You absolute bastard," he began.

"David, what a pleasant surprise. How can I help you?"

"You are the lowest scum I've ever met."

"Oh, come on, you're an MP, your bathe in effluence every day."

"Do you realise the trouble you're in? You have committed crimes that could put you away for years."

"Your word against mine. I'll say you gave the files to me."

"What have you seen? And why the hell would I do that?"

"I've seen everything that's on your computer. I'll say you had a few drinks and started boasting about what a big slapper you are, how they trust you with secrets, like the Hugh Dillsburgh affair. Good tabloid-y stuff."

A pause. I knew his testicles were disappearing into his body and a cold sweat was forming pleasingly on his forehead as the implications sunk into his sludge. I allowed a few seconds for the fear to take root. He was so easy to hornswoggle.

"You're just trying to wreck things between Lizzie and I."

"You're perfectly capable of doing that without my assistance, David. This is about Hugh Dillsburgh. I want you to tell me about the weapons. And Ocean Investment."

A pause. He was trying to work out what the hell was happening.

"But why would you want to know? You're a failed academic in a second rate toilet of a university. You're not a political animal."

He was completely baffled. It was a pleasant sensation for me. On the other hand I needed to cover myself so that he wouldn't know about Rook Investigations.

"It's personal. A dear friend of mine lost her husband and he was somehow in cahoots with

Dillsburgh. When he died she was terrified it wasn't an accident and something might happen to her and her family. I need to reassure her. That's all I need."

"And if I tell you to sod off?"

"I send all your computer files to a newspaper. Then you'll be begging for a post as a failed academic in a second rate toilet of a university. Given that you won't be a political animal any more. Give me at least some of the story then I'll know what to tell her. Don't lie, because I'll know."

"You're insane. This is classified. Official secrets."

"It won't be so secret once everyone knows and you make the front page of *The Sun*."

He tried to find a way out, but there wasn't one. He was too self-important to take a risk.

"OK. When we were in power Dillsburgh set up an illegal arms trade with insurrectionists in Afghanistan. It had approval but he went much further – personnel as well as arms. It was also lucrative for him. To be honest, there was a lot of relief when he died."

"OK. I believe you. Suppose it was neither an accident nor suicide?"

"Then your friend needs to be careful. Someone is out there with a grudge, though God knows who, or why."

"OK David. That will be all."

"Rot in hell. What about my files?"

"They're safe."

I ended the call. Now I had real information. And I'd kept Rook Investigations in the shade. I was tired, a little drunk, my daughter was furious with me, my career was on hold, my ex-wife hated me, I'd just thrown out my best friend, but I felt damned good and I had a parrot who liked me. The glass was half full, in this case with scotch.

Chapter XV

'Only the dead have seen the end of war.'

Plato

I booked a flight to Prague, and then filled in a university fees and expenses form to claim the money. Audrey's response would be interesting. It was a sunny morning; my office was filled with light and you could see galaxies in the swirling dust motes. Alfred was on the window sill looking out at the sky and muttering to himself. I wondered if he dreamed of freedom and what he might do with it. I'd miss him. I had a seminar about to begin and Anna's funeral afterwards.

Cass remained sultry and uncommunicative throughout the seminar. As the students trooped out I called her back. She came and stood by my desk, pointedly not looking at me.

"I'm sorry. I overreacted," I said.

"How do you think I feel?"

"I don't know. Tell me."

"It's a bit late for that. You always listen when it's too late. Sometimes I think how impossible it must have been for Mum. You keep everything in. Words are smokescreens for you. Sometimes I just long for you to say, simply, without irony, what you feel."

Alfred turned from the window and said in a voice alarmingly like mine: "If anything happened to Cass the world would end. I love her so much, Alfred, yet I rarely tell her. What kind of fuckwit am I? I'd do anything for her."

Cass and I looked at each other, both surprised. Alfred did a little jig, then said: "But how can I be so stupid with my own daughter? When I love her so much."

There was a pause as this sunk in, and then Cass exploded with laughter and hugged me. I winked at Alfred. It was alright. Where I singularly failed with my own daughter, a parrot had succeeded spectacularly. Clearly, I could learn a lot from him on how to conduct relationships. Now the ice had melted between us, Cass was keen to help with the case. I was equally keen for her not to, given the body count. I gave her something to do which I thought might help flush out our killer but keep her in the background. I gave her thirty pounds to buy a cheap mobile phone, register it under a false name, send me an anonymous message asking to meet me about Ocean Investment, and then destroy the phone. She left much happier than when she came in. An hour later I received a text: *Meet me this evening at 8 pm. Highgate tube. Priory Gdns exit. Ocean Investment.* The road ended in a cul-de-sac at the station so traffic could only approach and leave one way. And it was an entrance easy to observe. I hoped this might flush out Gladiator if he fell for it. I was still in a fog over this case, but at least I was moving and you might bump into someone in a fog. I also got a call from Mary King saying she needed to see me.

As I left the university Ron was hiding behind a wheelie bin ready to ambush me. "Paul, I've been thinking," he said.

"A dangerous habit which you should discard immediately. If you're not used to it then it might become addictive and pretty soon you'll come to realise that most things are futile and suicide is the best option. Sometimes the only one."

"But I've realised I should be open to new experiences," he said.

"OK. Good luck, Ron."

"So I'm prepared to bite the bullet."

"Right."

"I've booked a hotel. Friday. Just outside Milton Keynes."

"Ron, I have to go."

"Away from prying eyes. We don't want gossip."

"I don't know what you're talking about."

"You kissed me. I'd never thought of you that way, but I understand now what you were saying with that kiss. And after a lifetime of occasional heterosexual activity with my wife, I'm prepared to cross a new frontier. It might be just what I need."

He closed his eyes and puckered out his wet fishy lips for another kiss. What on earth was behind the hideous door I'd inadvertently opened in him?

"Ron, I only kissed you to shut you up. To stop you blathering on about your drab, pointless problems."

He looked crestfallen. He wanted to cross a frontier and it turned out to be another 'Stop' sign, one of many in his life, I imagined.

"But the hotel was forty nine pounds, dinner optional. I thought we'd go Dutch."

"Keep the hotel. Look." I looked up a number in my phone. "Ring this number and ask for Roxy. She's a good time girl. Tell her you want the full monty. She'll charge you fifty quid and it'll do you a damn sight more good than I could."

I left him looking at the number. I meet a lot of strange people in my line. Roxy is a nice girl. She'd be kind to Ron and be glad of the money.

*

The funeral was appalling. I sat at the back of the anonymous crematorium a few miles from Solihull, where Anna's family still lived. Piped music. Sanitised. Death-in-its-Sunday-best. I counted forty two people, probably mostly family. I suspect that Anna had been a mystery to her parents and an absence in their lives. She had rarely spoken of them. She left home and that was it. I don't think she even went back at Christmas. No one knew me there, of course. Nor did anyone ask who I was. Her mother was stoically shrouded in a black coat and hat and gloves, like a giant crow, and her father was eviscerated in his bones. I imagined being at Cass's funeral and knew I would fall apart, as he was doing.

The priest said that Anna, who had never shown the faintest interest in anything religious, had always loved Psalm twenty three. It is beautiful, and I say that as one who finds the idea of God gratuitously offensive and an affront to human intelligence. Her father's lips followed the words tremblingly: *The Lord is my shepherd; I shall not want*. I felt I should go to him and say, 'Your daughter was a beautiful young woman who deserved far better than me. It is my fault she is dead and anything you say or do will be less than I deserve.' *Yea, though I walk through the valley of the shadow of death, I will fear no evil: for thou art with me; thy rod and thy staff they comfort me. Thou preparest a table before me in the presence of mine enemies: thou anointest my head with oil; my cup runneth over.*

I put a hand to my cheek and to my surprise it was wet. The world in front of me blurred with tears. As I left I took out the little shell I'd taken from her flat and the bloody hair in the plastic envelope and made a promise. *Anna, I will find him. I will never stop until I have hunted him down.*

Chapter XVI

'Success is the ability to go from one failure to another with no loss of enthusiasm.'
Winston Churchill

The drive back to London was bleak. The world was full of rain. I wished I had better news to give to Mary King. I just had time to meet her at Marylebone before going to Highgate station. She bought me a coffee and we sat at the table where we'd first met. She looked under a lot of strain. There were faint blue patches under her eyes that hadn't been there before. I decided against telling her the death count was accruing. There was no point in alarming her further. I assumed she wanted an update. She touched the cut on my cheek.

"Goes with the job," I said. "I have a few leads and I'm going to Prague in the hope of finding more. Andy was involved in illegal arms deals."

"That's what I thought," she said.

I looked at her. How did she know and if she knew, why hadn't she told me? She gave me a plastic bag. Inside were six sheets of paper with a child's drawings on one side and on the other photographs of hi-tech weapons: Armatix Digital Revolver; KAC M110 Sniper Rifle; XM25 Smart Grenade; Launcher Magpul FMG-9 and others, some of which are still supposedly in the prototype phase. With global spending of nearly two hundred billion dollars on weapons every year, who knows what is being illegally tested by the rich on the world's poor? There were dates on each sheet, roughly three weekly intervals since January of last year.

"I found these under my son's bed this morning. Andy must have given them to him. They're all printed on our home computer, so I know they were Andy's."

On one of the sheets was a biro-written address in Prague. I would bet my house, if I still had one, that

I would find Ocean Investment there. She gave me a crumpled notebook.

"I also found this in Andy's things. He'd hidden it in the lining of an old sports bag."

A small notebook. A lot of doodles and horse racing notes. On the last page a heading: OCEAN SHIPMENTS PRAGUE TO AFGHANISTAN and a list of dates, which matched the dates on the weapons sheets. There were also three phone numbers. One I recognised as being Jimmy the Stump's.

"This is very helpful," I said.

She laid her right hand on my left.

"I want this to be over," she said. "It gets to me badly."

"Me too. And listen, from now on I don't want paying."

She looked at me curiously.

"Personal reasons," I said.

"Are there always personal reasons?"

"I started doing this work in the hope of finding my father. It's a long story. Another time."

"I hope you find him. But find Andy's killer first."

We stood and she kissed me lightly on the cheek. She smelled of lavender and almonds. She looked at me closely and then kissed me again, this time on the lips, a feather stroke of tenderness and wanting.

"When I said I wanted this to be over, I also meant…"

"I know," I said.

There was something very sexy about her mix of vulnerability and forwardness. She also had wonderful legs, which I watched as she walked away. I had no intention of anything happening during this investigation, and even afterwards it would doubtless be a mistake. It usually is.

*

I sat in my car in Priory Gardens, parked behind a camper van but still with a good view of Highgate station entrance. It was dark and raining but the entrance was well lit. The coffee caravan on the left was closed. I could see anyone who arrived or left. The only places for someone to watch, other than the station entrance, would be from a house or behind the closed coffee van, or from a car. Clusters of commuters came out, then a pause, then more commuters. I scanned faces looking for someone who was also looking for someone. At ten minutes past eight I decided to try and make something happen. There was a waste bin near the entrance to the station. I rolled up a newspaper and got out of my car, walked to the bin, looked around as if I was expecting someone, then pretended to take a call on my mobile, and put the newspaper in the bin. I walked down the concrete steps and turned left as if going into the station, but stopped and turned. I waited a few moments, and then peered around the corner. No one. I ducked back and waited a minute, then looked again. Someone in a hooded blue bomber jacket, wearing gloves and loose jeans, had just retrieved the paper from the bin and was turning away. I started up the steps but some instinct told them – they half turned and then ran. I ran up the steps after them. It was dark and I got no glimpse of a face.

Twenty yards down the road they got in the same black BMW I'd seen the day before. The car was facing the right way and the engine must have been left running because they were away in a second. I ran back to my car but by the time I'd got in and turned the car around, I knew it was too late. Damn it. If only they had turned another fraction at the station I might have glimpsed a face. However this time I did get a number plate. MRW 309B.

As soon as I got back to the flat I traced the number plate on the DVLA website. It was a hire car firm. I rang them and pretended to be the hirer and that I'd lost the keys, but they asked a few security questions and then put down the phone. I phoned the two numbers in Andy's notebook. The first was dead. On the second I got lucky. A voicemail message: "This is Hugh. Please leave a message after the tone." The inimitable tone of a self-important politician which I recognised from such comedy programmes as *Newsnight* and *Question Time*. Hugh Dillsburgh. Now I had the connection between him and Andy King.

The next day I got a new mobile. Hopefully this one wouldn't be hacked. Not for the first time in this investigation I was completely wrong. A text beeped: *Thanks for the newspaper. Congrats on new phone. Be in touch soon. Gladiator.* In the afternoon I was flying to Prague. I decided to call in on Mum first to see if she'd rallied any more. Seeing Anna's parents had made me think of Cass, but also about my own parents, including my father, wherever he was. If he was. As I approached Mum's room I could hear her talking. She sounded animated and almost sane.

"Back when it was proper sterrer. Sterilised milk. Creamy. And the milkman came in for a Christmas drink. Whisky. Kept his cap on. Moustache. Like that one with the cane bend over boy whatshisname Jammy Edwards that's it."

Symon was with her. He was smiling at her and turned to me. No reaction. No flicker of guilt.

"She's positively garrulous," he said. "Real chat we're having, eh?"

She smiled at him then looked at me as if I was a complete stranger. I felt an irrational jealousy that this shadow from my past could turn up after a lifetime and charm my senile mother into smiles and conversation of sorts. I swallowed the feeling, kissed Mum on the cheek and sat. I noticed that a few moments later she wiped her cheek with a tissue. Symon noticed too. Ten minutes later I stood and said we had to go, looking at Symon. He took the hint.

Outside I turned on him.

"What the hell are you doing? Turn up out of the blue and somehow animate Mum, but what happens when you sail away? I can't do that. I'm in for the long haul."

"I thought you'd be pleased," he said.

"I am, you bastard. That's why I'm so angry."

"This is really about Cass, isn't it?"

"Of course it is. And I know nothing happened. I just want to savour the feeling of self-righteous fatherly indignation for a few more moments."

He smiled. Friendships shouldn't be complicated like marriages, but this one seemed to be.

"Actually I had an ulterior motive in coming to see your mum. I know she won't say anything about your dad to you, but I thought she might to me."

"And did she?"

"No. But she might."

"Pigs will fly."

We walked to our cars.

"Any developments?" he asked.

"Yes. A few. But quite honestly, I think I'm better solo."

"Understood. Let me know if you do want me to do anything."

"I will."

"I am your friend, you know, Paul. From what I've seen, just about the only one."

"I have Cass and a thousand dead voices. Oh, and Alfred."

"Who's Alfred?"

"A friend."

And so we parted. Difficult waters negotiated. He saw my small flight bag packed in the back of my car but asked nothing. I remembered again that this was one of the things I had always liked about him – he respected my need to keep secrets. When we were kids I convinced him I had the most precious object in the world, something I'd always craved, and it was hidden in the tiny cellar of our flat. He longed to pull the flap open and go down there, but never did. I pretended I'd gone out once, so I could see if he would satisfy his curiosity, and I watched through a crack in the kitchen door as he came from our little front room, looked down at the cellar flap, then went back and sat down. That's when I knew he was a friend. Of course, I'd fabricated it all and there was nothing in the cellar. There never is.

Chapter XVII

'What is reality? Is it not merely a term for the philosopher to conjure with, behind which he may craftily conceal his ignorance?'

John Grier Hibben

The next day I called in at the university to cancel a few things and check on Alfred. He was having a coffee break with Mrs. Simpson.

"This Alfred is more clever than 'alf the people working 'ere, Dr Rook," she said.

"I agree, Mrs. Simpson. The trouble is that's not much of a compliment. There's you and Alfred and I, and a lot of dead wood. And the new Head of Department, Audrey, is to thinking what Sweeney Todd was to hairdressing."

"She shouldn't wear stripes. Not with those hips. Some are alright 'ere. Mr Spinks in catering. 'E's a good 'ead for figures, even with 'is gammy leg," she said. "I think 'e wanted to be a paratrooper, but that bloody leg."

"I think therefore I am," said Alfred, repeating another snippet he'd heard. Sometimes a single word would trigger a remembered phrase for him.

A knock on the door and it opened and Mary King entered. She looked particularly sumptuous, I thought, in a red woollen dress and short black jacket. I knew she'd thought carefully about what to wear and, ludicrously, I was flattered. Mrs. Simpson was agog and sensed a something in the air.

"Mrs. Simpson. This is Mary. A friend."

"I see," said Mrs. Simpson, barely avoiding a nudge-nudge-wink, "I'll leave you to it then," and left with a knowing smile at Mary.

"How did you know where to find me?" I asked.

"You told me about your day job. I'm sorry, I know it's against the rules but there was something else I had to tell you."

She looked nervous, even flustered. I made coffee and she sipped it, looking at Alfred, who had hopped to the window sill and was nibbling thoughtfully on a crispbread, watching us. I gave her a moment.

"Andy knew something was up. He wasn't bright but he had feeling. He said he felt he was in danger. The thing is, and I can't forgive myself for it, I told him he was being stupid. The next delivery was for a lot of money and I saw it as our way out, our meal ticket to Fiji. A new life. I sent him to his death and I needed to tell you that."

Her eyes filled. I don't do grief counselling, not my job, but before I knew it I'd taken her hand.

"No. You didn't kill him. Don't beat yourself up."

"I sent him to his death," said Alfred in a perfect imitation of Mary's voice. She was taken by surprise and almost spilled her coffee.

"He does that. He's a perfect mimic," I said.

"Creepy," she said.

"I've grown fond of him, He belonged to Jimmy Mullins."

"I haven't said anything. I don't know anything. Just go away. Please. No, no." Alfred said in a perfect and moving simulation of Jimmy's voice.

She clearly found Alfred too much, as if her grief was being mocked. I told her I was going to Prague and would let her know the outcome, as soon as there was one, and she left. At the door she kissed me lightly on the cheek. I almost held her close. I expected Alfred to wolf whistle, but he didn't. I wondered if Mary's children would like me. I would probably find them annoying, but Mary had wonderful legs.

*

At Gatwick airport I was sure I was being watched. Everywhere was eyes. The same man sitting near me in Costa Coffee was standing next to me in Dixons as I looked at the tablets and iPods and machines that all spoke to each other and were recreating the world into a jungle of barcodes and gratuitous communication. A two thousand pound dark grey suit. Expensive brown brogues. Short cropped greying hair, rimless steel spectacles. Already I didn't like him. He looked like a Nazi dentist. I turned to him and said, "Choice is a bad thing. It confuses me."

He smiled and nodded in agreement. I wanted to hear his voice.

"Going far?" I asked.

"Dubai," he said.

"Business or pleasure?"

"Business is pleasure. When it's going well."

Then he walked away. Mid-West American. Money. He was also lying. He had a carrier bag with what looked like a brand new pair of fleece lined gloves inside. Dubai had current temperatures of up to thirty one degrees centigrade. I don't think so, America.

*

Prague appeals to my imagination. Ancient, iconoclastic, cultured, embittered, like an old scholar warrior nursing his grudges. It has irony too, leaving the Russian tanks in its streets to both rot and remember. A city has many realities, like a hydra, and in Prague they are often in silent dispute. Ice Age hunters, warring Germanic, Celtic and Slavic tribes that carved an unruly history in the cradle of Bohemia and which, thousands of years later, now peer from the shadows at a current burgeoning tourism and a boilingly corrupt City Hall. It makes me feel barbaric, civilized and litigious. You can walk off the streets and hear a string quartet to break the heart of Vlad the Impaler.

I booked into the Marriott hotel. I suppered on a bag of peanuts, two glasses of heavy Rioja and a Famous Grouse, then strolled out and past the building several doors along. This was it. I stopped and looked at the nameplates, then photographed them with my mobile. I walked on to the Old Town Square, looked up at the astronomical clock, and spent five minutes watching a fire eater in the streets. She was a young woman of about twenty eight with Nordic pigtails and wide dark eyes, muffled inside a thick jumpsuit against the cold, but with a cloak of black and gold to add a touch of Wicca and theatre. She held one flaming sword aloft and the other she twirled with her left hand. Then she looked up at the blackening sky and lowered the sword into her mouth. She kept it there, and then slowly removed it – extinguished and smoking, to gentle applause.

I flipped two Korunas into a copper pot and she smiled.

"Speak English?" I asked.

"A little," she said.

"You do this because you like risk?" I asked.

"Everything important is a risk, so I do this to remind me. You like to try?"

"Sure," I said.

I liked the whiff of danger about it. She said that the trick is to remember that fire and hot air travel up, so keep the sword angled properly and tilt your head, flatten the tongue and above all, don't inhale, otherwise you set fire to your lungs. Then exhale to douse the flame. When you are frightened your throat constricts, so take a few deep breaths beforehand and try to relax. I learnt a long time ago that fear is about choice. There is a moment when you decide to do something, not because you've conquered your fear, but because you choose to ignore it and take that unknown leap anyway. She gave me a flaming sword. I could smell petrol. I took a few breaths, raised the sword, faced skyward, and opened my mouth. I could feel the heat on my face but kept lowering the sword into my mouth, the flames rippling up the dulled blade. When it reached the back of my throat I exhaled as quickly as I could. The flames spluttered out but I breathed in and got a mouthful of fumes and petrol. I spat on the ground but held the sword aloft. A few passers-by applauded and the young woman shouted "Bravo!"

An hour later I sat in my hotel room and charged two new mobile phones I'd brought with me, then did an internet search on my laptop of all the businesses listed on the nameplate that I had photographed. All were readily available except one. Caneo Inc. No trace anywhere. Caneo is an anagram of Ocean. This was it. After a restless night of dreams full of fire and Anna and then seeing Lizzie waving at me from the other shore of a wide turbulent river, I woke up sweating and hyperventilating. I didn't need a shrink to work out some of the ramifications of that little night of vipers. I left the hotel and went to the building where I knew Ocean Investment to be. I rang the Caneo strip and waited. Nothing. I waited until someone, a middle aged man in a suit, arrived to go to one of the other offices.

"*Dobry den. Mluvite Ingles?*" I asked.

"A little English," he said.

"Great. Can you tell me where I can find Tourist Information?"

He gave me directions and I thanked him. He closed the door and I waited a few minutes, then keyed in the same code I'd watched him use. Caneo Inc. was on the fifth floor. I took the lift and got out. There were two companies on each floor. This had Caneo and an Insurance company, Baranek. Their office hadn't opened yet. I tried the door of Caneo but it was locked and there was a code punch by the door. I looked around – no CCTV, which was lucky.

I sat on the stairs and thought. I took out Andy's little notebook and flipped through it again. The dates at the back were, I assumed, dates of arms shipments. The last date had no slashes between the numbers to indicate days and month. I tried it on the code pad. Wrong. I rang Mary and asked her for Andy's birth date and her own, and those of her children. I tried them all, praying that the pad didn't have a disabling trip switch which shut it down after a certain number of errors. I tried Mary's first, then Andy's and there was a click and the door opened.

Inside was not what I expected. It was dusty, unused, a smell of deadness and abandonment. A reception area with a bare wooden floor and scraps of newspaper like vagrant place mats. Mice or rats had been colonising the place. There were two offices left and right with only desks in. One had a pile of folders. I looked through them. Bizarrely they were mostly full of carpet samples – I assumed from the previous tenant.

Behind the reception area was a larger office. Desk, chair, filing cabinet. I looked in the desk. Some weapons catalogues. In another drawer old flight tickets and travel itineraries: Mr Andrew

Thomas King, at least a dozen flights from Prague to Istanbul, then a return flight from Kabul to Prague via Istanbul. There were other documents – invoices from car hire companies in Istanbul. A picture began to emerge. I speculated that this was where Andy would come to arrange money transfers, and then he would go to Istanbul, where perhaps the weapons would be collected, then taken either overland or by private charter, which was more likely, to Kabul. Then he would fly back. I had thought that Andy was little more than a mule, albeit a crucial one, but he started to go up in my estimation as I read through some emails that had been printed off, with headings such as 'Avoiding Surveillance'; 'Code names for suppliers'; 'Details for changing overland routes.'

The filing cabinet was locked. I found a screwdriver in the desk drawer and prised it open. A few Xerox files of weapons and consignments, a bundle of receipts from restaurants and taxis. At the back a list of contacts. This made it worth the journey. Hugh Dillsburgh, two other MPs, some

MOD Personnel, Special Branch, all with code names. Dillsburgh, hilariously, was MOUSE. Then the one I was looking for. GLADIATOR. No name but a phone number. I used one of my new mobiles and rang the number.

"Yes?"

I stopped the call, dropped the phone and stamped it dead. The voice was Symon Crace's. I sat down and looped my mind back. I'd been so stupid, so gullible. Symon's fortuitous and sudden reappearance in my life just as I took this investigation; his apparently nomadic, homeless existence; his innocuous ability to gain my trust; questions about the investigation; the endless texting and philosophical conundrums. I took the hair I had found under Anna's nail from the little plastic wallet that I carried in my pocket. There was a tiny galley kitchen and I held the hair under the tap. The blood had stained it red but it lightened a little – this could easily have been a blonde hair. Symon's. What had I told him? Too much, of course. Far too much. He'd been playing me all along while killing off anyone I came close to. I could speculate on why he killed Andy King, if King was street bragging about the arms deals, but all the others? Had there been some big falling out? What was he still hiding? Presumably a trail that would lead to him as a main player in an International illegal arms trade. I was spitting angry. I'd let him live in my flat. He'd murdered Anna. My own daughter had fallen for his wayward, lying charm. Cass, Cass. I feared the worst and phoned her.

"It's Dad. Where are you?"

"At home. Are you OK?"

"Yes. Listen, if Symon contacts you..."

"He's here. He just popped in to collect a few things."

My heart squeezed into a ball. God, I prayed she didn't have the phone in conference mode.

"Cass. This is very important. Please don't ask any questions. Act normally. Thirty seconds after this call I will ring again. Pretend it's a friend, or

Mum, and it's an emergency, and you have to leave immediately. You have to do this."

"Dad, you're scaring me."

"Don't be scared. If you just do what I say you'll be fine. I love you."

I counted to thirty and rang back.

"Hello," she said, her voice thin.

"It's going to be fine. Leave now and don't tell Symon where you're going..."

Suddenly Symon's voice. "It's too late for that. Why couldn't you just play along? Why be so bloody complicated? This could have been easy."

"If you hurt her I'll kill you. I won't stop until I do. Just leave her," I said.

"Paul, this is not some crap movie. Don't threaten me. You don't have the substance for it. Cass will be safe with me. I'll be in touch. I know what I'm doing."

Then he was gone. I knew the knot in my stomach would only tighten until I was back in England and could find Cass. My Cass. Then I heard the main door to the offices open. I got down below the desk.

I could see a man's legs checking the other two small offices. Expensive brown brogues. America. If he came in here there was nowhere to hide. It seemed better to at least take the initiative and give myself the advantage of surprise. I stood and ran at him while he had his back turned. I barged into him and he fell heavily, but I kept my balance and ran out. No point in taking the lift, so I ran down the stairs. I got down three floors before I heard him coming after me. I opened the front door and slammed it behind me and ran.

When I reached the Old Town Square I knew I was almost done. My lungs had clearly shrunk to the size of a postage stamp. I was about as fit as a middle aged man who takes no exercise and drinks too much was entitled to be. There was my young sword swallowing friend. I ran up to her and put my arms around her, pulling her cloak around my back, and kissed her full on the lips. She tasted of petrol and mint. It was a long and lingering kiss. I saw from the corner of my eye the man I knocked over run into the square, stop and look around, then make a wrong decision and run diagonally across and away. I pulled away, breathless.

"I can't thank you enough," I said.

She looked amused and curious. I walked away. I had to get to Cass.

Chapter XVIII

'Burning for burning, wound for wound, stripe for stripe.'

Exodus 25

I counted clouds. I counted the windows in the plane. I counted the number of passengers. I closed my eyes and tried to count the flickering dots. I tried to recite some of the Old Testament just to remind me of how we need to shed this ludicrous, archaic religion. Indeed all religions. Even animals get punished in the Old Testament vision of things: "If the ox shall push a manservant or a maidservant; he shall give unto their master thirty shekels of silver, and the ox shall be stoned." Even that failed to distract. I twitched and sighed and fretted my way through the flight. Symon could gain nothing from murdering Cass. His kills were functional – to either stop someone from talking to me or from passing on what I may have said to them. If Anna's death was merely a warning, this made it far more chilling, but would he kill Cass too? Had something been unleashed in him that couldn't be reined in? And beneath all this was a nag of uncertainty about everything. I tried meditating but thought that if the Buddha was on an EasyJet Boeing 737, seething with revenge fantasies, a slight hangover and wondering what the hell his murdering former best friend was going to do to his daughter, then the smile might twist a little, and the paunch become dyspeptic. I felt physically sick and when the man next to me tucked into an evil smelling bacon sandwich I almost gagged over his cheap suit. He looked shocked when I turned to him and said, "Do you mind troughing that greasy slop a bit more quietly? You sound like an unplugged drain."

I drove like a demon from Gatwick. At best I was hoping that he would have relented and left Cass in the flat, though I knew that unlikely. I tried her number and his, but it went straight to voicemail. At the flat there was no message. Nothing. Everything about this investigation had been twisted and circuitous. I telephoned Mary King and told her I knew who her husband's killer was, a man called Symon Crace, and that I would doubtless be seeing him soon. I had long decided not to tell her where she could find her husband's killer in case she had some dangerous revenge fantasy that would end in her being the victim, but she didn't ask. It was enough to know who it was. To have a name to curse, as she had first said to me. She told me to be careful. Then my landline rang. Symon, telling me to come to an address in North London, an industrial estate by the River Lea. I said I'd be there in an hour, trying to keep the panic and murderous fury out of my voice. I had to keep a lid on my mind, which was now a williwaw of scorpions, if I was to be of use to Cass. I don't think I've ever hated anyone as much as I hated Symon at that moment. I should have known. Someone said that behind every fortune is a crime, and Symon had been at great pains to tell me how wealthy he was.

"Let me speak to Cass," I said.

Moments later. "Dad. Please come soon."

"Hang on. I love you."

Just as I was leaving the phone rang again.

"Dr Rook. Audrey Pritchard. You are meant to be at a sub-committee meeting for Creating a Safe Learning Environment. Where are you?"

"You've just rung my home number so it's pretty bloody obvious where I am."

"I am making a formal complaint about you for unprofessional behaviour, dereliction of duties and illegally keeping a creature on university premises."

"And I'm making a complaint about you simply for being you. In fact I am going to call a meeting in order to challenge for your position."

I then wrote an email to Lizzie, telling her everything that had happened, about Rook Investigations, how sorry I was for being me, how I would always love her, and as much as I knew about Symon, and Mary King's contact details. I put it on a delay timer so that unless I was able to delete it within twelve hours it would send automatically. It was a small and cruel insurance, but desperation creates its own road. And she deserved some truth. I took out the hair in the little plastic envelope. My mind started to snag on details, uncertainties. Then I left.

*

The industrial park was mostly abandoned workshops and storage units. I parked outside unit 32. There were no other cars – Symon must have parked off-road somewhere. It was dark because most of the security lights had long since dimmed or been vandalised. The unit door was closed. I knocked. It opened straight away.

"Get inside," said Symon. He held a silver automatic revolver and a small torch in the other hand. I entered; he took a quick look around outside and closed the door behind us. He led me along a small corridor and opened a door into a windowless box room. Cass stood and rushed to my arms. I held her, breathed the pine and rosemary of her hair, smelled her fear, and whispered that everything was going to be fine. Her eyes filled. She shook in my arms. I turned to face Symon and wanted to kill him.

"Why?" I asked.

"Tell me what you think you know," he said.

"You retiring from a successful business was a lie. In fact everything about the way you represented yourself is a lie. You're a gun running psychopath on a murder spree. What makes me spitting angry, though, is that you've frightened my daughter and you killed someone close to me who wasn't connected with your grubby little death trade."

"Someone close to you?" said Cass, suddenly anxious about Lizzie.

"Anna."

Cass looked at Symon. "You're a monster."

Symon sat and took a deep breath.

"Now you've had your cathartic moment, let me tell you both what really happened. No, I wasn't a businessman. I worked in Security for ten years, and then made a killing, no pun, in Iraq when the British and American governments were more than happy to throw money at people like me. It was a gravy train. The winners in that war were mercenaries and oil barons. We called ourselves security contractors but we were private armies. Two of us to every six soldiers. You've no idea how much money we were making. My company got a 100 mill contract protecting oil fields so that the US and UK barons could rob from them, plus regular five mill sweeteners creamed off reconstruction money. Legal lines blurred as aid money was arguably as much ours as anyone's. It was a truly privatised war. Plus mercenaries could kill anyone – rivals, imagined rivals, protesters, activists – anyone, and because of the great global terror scam our arses were always covered. I became the weapons man – supplying state of the art firepower to other companies. I was making over two hundred grand a week."

"Very noble. And then you did the same in Afghanistan?"

"Yes. Some protection of bases, but the US and UK governments also paid me to arm 'kill teams' – special forces that work at night, going into villages to assassinate Afghan fighters who oppose the occupation, and to terrorize civilians who might harbour them."

"These aren't regular soldiers?"

"Not many soldiers at all. A few ex-commandos, but mostly mercenaries who combine greed for money with a hunger to kill. Dillsburgh was the main man in the government who channelled the funds, and he continued this in Opposition. Callous, ruthless bastard."

"Not a liberal humanitarian like you then?" I said.

Symon smiled.

"He was just the sort Blair and Bush liked to do their dirty work while they could pretend they knew nothing about it. You won't believe me but I grew sick of it. I didn't care about the politics. I expect them to be corrupt. But the body counts were becoming huge. I wanted out."

"But they wouldn't let you out."

"There is no out. Not in my game. Stakes are too high."

"Where did Andy King come in?"

"He was a mistake. Knew it the first time I met him. Chancer. Big mouth, but hell could he plan. The documentation was superb. Travel itineraries, evasive techniques, bureaucratic quagmires ploughed through to buy weapons. But he started to brag."

"So he had to be wiped out."

"Disappeared. Dillsburgh gave me the order. Our operations were so big, so global, that we were starting to be less discriminating about who we employed. Big mistake."

"Where did Jimmy Mullins and Rod Whiteley fit in?"

"Mullins was the initial contact. He'd been approached and had vouched for King as a good risk taker. He didn't really know what we were about. Whiteley also vouched for King. He got a commission for everyone he recommended, so he wasn't fussy. We were really starting to drag the bottom of the pond for people."

"So directly or indirectly, recruitment was targeted at known felons?"

"That's right. The thing about using criminals is that most of them knew to keep their mouths shut and some we could blackmail if they got too out of line. Trouble is, nobody quite knew where the lines were any more."

"So then when King started to become a liability you were told to kill anyone associated with him. Just in case they knew something. In case they talked."

Symon took a deep breath. Suddenly he looked a tired and ageing man. The ebullience, the boyish sangfroid, evaporated.

"Paul, I didn't kill them. I shot King. Dillsburgh I assumed was a heart attack or a stroke at the wheel. Who knows? Jimmy Mullins, Rod Whiteley, Anna. Not guilty M'Lud."

"Then who killed them?" asked Cass.

Symon shrugged.

"The text messages. The philosophical puzzles, the mind games, knowing where I was," I said.

"Not me. Whoever he is, he's scarily good."

Symon said that once Dillsburgh was dead he thought the operation was in jeopardy. No one quite knew who was now 'officially' in charge. He'd had Mary King's phone tapped when he was preparing to kill Andy and as insurance to see if she might be trouble. That's how he knew she'd contacted me. He couldn't believe it at first when my name came up. Then she changed her number. He came to my place to find out her intentions – the fear was that if she knew anything about what King had been up to she might go to the media, but then the killing started and he thought someone either in the military or in government had ordered a clampdown. Every now and then there was a spring cleaning of personnel in companies such as his, if anything started to get messy. It was a ruthless global business. There seemed to be a cull of anyone associated with King, and that might include Symon himself, given that he'd voiced dissent, so he needed to find the killer. What better place to be than with the investigator who was also trying to find him?

"Believe it or not, I also thought I might be able to protect you. That's why I tried to throw you off the Ocean Investment scent. If you thought it was a dead end you might throw the case and then you'd be safe. I brought Cass here to protect her."

I looked at Symon.

"I know it wasn't you who killed them all," I said.

He looked shocked. "Then why all the questions?"

"I still thought Cass might be in danger. And I wasn't absolutely sure."

His phone trilled. He looked at it, then showed me a text: *You next.* No number. I could tell from Cass's expression that she didn't believe him and thought this might be a set up. I did believe him. I knew now. I should have put together all the pieces before.

Chapter XIX

'All grandeur, all power, and all subordination to authority rests on the executioner: he is the horror and the bond of human association. Remove this incomprehensible agent from the world and at that very moment order gives way to chaos, thrones topple and society disappears.'

Joseph De Maistre

"So what now, James Bond?" I asked.

Symon looked at me.

"I wish I knew. It's a mistake to go back to your place. If this cull is a big operation involving the military, and behind that government, trying to cover its tracks, then our only outside chance is to disappear. I know how to do that. It'll cost, but I have a lot of money."

Cass looked at me, alarmed.

"Dad. We can't."

"We won't," I said.

Symon turned on me.

"You don't know what you're dealing with, Paul. Please listen to me! Just trying to go on as normal will leave you both dead."

But already my mind was working in another direction. A speculation was now a certainty. If I was right then it changed everything. I said that Cass and I were going back to the flat. Symon shook his head.

"I can't help you then," he said.

"You're the one who needs to be careful. Where will you go?"

"I can't tell you that. It might endanger you to know."

"There was a man in Prague who'd been following me. American Mid-West. Cropped grey hair. Natty dresser. Is he with you?"

"No. And that's why you should disappear, Paul. You could be OK but they might see you as loose ends, and none of these people like loose ends. This is a billion dollar business."

We walked out into a night milky with stars bright as dreams. A new moon offered its face in the inky infinity. A dread was in the chill air and I could almost see it coming before it happens. Cass ahead, me just to her left and Symon behind, walking towards our cars and goodbyes. The world is an angular kaleidoscope of shadows, then a cat movement of something else, the stealth of an assassin. The soft whoosh of a gun with a silencer. I turn and Symon walks another few steps then it is as if each layer of him gives way in turn. First the feet refuse, then the knees, and the rest of his body strangely goes forward as he collapses. His eyes still vivid in the night. I think he is dead before he hits the ground. Even so his lips part and it is as if his whole concentration is arched to pronounce a word, perhaps a syllable, and I strain to hear as I move towards him, but it is only a last breath, more a sigh, as if wearily wondering if it has all been worth the effort, just to reach this end in a cold bleak place. The night is like a trauma built of darkness.

Cass reacts as if in slow motion. It takes a full ten seconds for her to register what is happening. I wait for her to scream but she doesn't. Something collapses in her and she steps back, almost falling against my car. Now I see the black BMW parked in shadows a hundred metres away. Symon is gone into the night. I feel the silence in his neck with two of my fingers. I look up at the figure some ten metres away holding the gun. Black jogging bottoms, blue padded bomber jacket, balaclava, black gloves, turning to walk away to the car but stops with a jerk when I call the name.

"Mary."

The figure turns. A decision is made. She takes off the balaclava and shakes loose her hair. She half smiles. I've surprised her.

"Who's a clever boy then?" she says. "When did you know?"

"Alfred started it. He saw you and said Jimmy's last words. He'd seen you before. You said I'd told you where I taught and I knew I hadn't. And it made no sense that you were still alive, unless you were the killer. I just wish I'd tied it all together sooner. What now?"

"It's over. My work's done," she said.

"So you just walk away. Carnage but no regrets?"

"Something like that. I always liked you, Paul, despite your scruffy exterior. You were wearing that jacket ten years ago."

What did she mean? She registered my surprise.

"The Royal Institute of Philosophy. A series of public lectures: *The Idea of Crime in Secular Society*. Dr Paul Rook. Sitting at the back, a mousy little thing – before I dyed my hair – eagerly taking notes and definitely having a ridiculous schoolgirl crush on you. Full of feeling and aspirations."

"Jesus. That's where the philosophy interest came from. The cryptic texts."

"Yes, I was enchanted with you and all these years later I suppose I wanted to enchant you. I thought you'd understand what I was doing. I also chose you because I heard you were good. You could help find the people I had to get and who wouldn't see me. It was just a coincidence that one of them," she looked at what had been Symon, "...was your friend. Anyway, it's done now. I had to get the whole nest of vipers. Anyone connected with Andy's death. Jimmy got him into it. Whiteley vouched for him. None of them deserved to live. Natural Law."

Suddenly I understood.

"You're dressing it up as retribution, but it's guilt."

Her eyes sharpened. Malice waiting to be triggered.

"Don't be too clever, Paul. Let it go."

"Dad, let's leave," said Cass.

"It was you. Andy wasn't clever enough but you were. You did the arms deals, the distribution, the contacts. Andy really was just the mule. But everyone thought it was him and you were just good little wifey at home. And he got killed for it all. So now you want to try and assuage your guilt in a heap of dead bodies."

"Dad!" shouted Cass.

"It's all right, Cass. Like most nutters, she has a weird logic. We weren't in any way responsible for Andy's death, so to kill us would be against her perverted code. But why Anna? She had nothing to do with it."

"A mistake. You were her lover. People say a lot in bed. I had to know if you'd said anything that might be useful to me."

This didn't quite make sense. She could see I knew that.

"Plus, I was jealous. I wanted to know what sort of woman you went for. She was haughty, dismissive, a stuck up bitch and she tried to throw me out. Things got out of hand and I suddenly got so angry. I'm sorry."

"Mary, do you have any idea just how loony tunes you are?"

Something shifted behind her eyes, some prehensile loathing, some creature of the night flitting through, leaving its bloody footprints.

"This is your last chance. Leave with your daughter now."

"One last question: how did you keep track of me? I found the device in the car."

"I put another one in you."

What the hell did she mean?

"Miniature GPS tracking device. Only available thought the military. Stays in the human system a few days. Don't worry. It won't harm you. And I won't be doing it again."

I quickly flipped through all our meetings. How had she done it?

"Coffee. Every time I saw you we had coffee. That's how you did it."

She nodded. Suddenly her face darkened again.

"Go," she said.

I had a hundred other questions. I had another dead friend. I also had a daughter who needed me. I'd put her at such risk. I looked down at Symon. Mary did too. Then she looked at me.

"Make an anonymous call to the police. You're an old hand at that. And he doesn't care if you stay or go. Great thing about the dead – they don't make a fuss. If you get involved it will get very messy for you. They'll question you soon enough if they discover you were connected."

I opened my car door. Cass was already in the passenger seat. I turned and Mary gave a small ironic wave. She assumed we wouldn't meet again, but I was already making other plans. I took out my phone and cancelled the timed email to Lizzie.

Chapter XX

'Reality is merely an illusion, albeit a very persistent one.'

Albert Einstein

Cass was in shock. I made her a mug of tea and put a triple brandy in it.

"He was your friend. He lived with us. I cared about him and he died trying to help us and we just left him like a piece of rubbish," she said.

Cass was expecting me to justify it with some abstruse argument. I didn't. There was no point.

"Yes. We did. And now it's done and we have to live with it. Cass, it's too dangerous for you to be involved with Rook Investigations. It has to stop."

She looked at me tearfully.

"I knew you'd say that. But I know about it. I can't un-know."

We stirred the argument up a little but she didn't have the heart to sustain it. "I want you to go to your Mum's for a while. Just until this is over."

She turned on me. "But it is over."

"Not yet. There's a big full stop missing."

*

The next morning I dropped a reluctant Cass at Lizzie's. I promised we'd do something for Symon. A private little ceremony all of our own. She seemed to find comfort in this. I didn't go in, though I did register Lizzie looking daggers at me from the door. Then I went to the university, made a large pot of coffee and locked the door. Alfred preened his feathers and sensed the need for thought.

"I think therefore I am," he said.

"Quite right, old buddy," I said.

"They that had fought so well
Came thro' the jaws of Death,
Back from the mouth of Hell,"

I finished the verse.

"All that was left of them,

Left of six hundred."

I got down to serious profiling. I don't do conventional profiling, more a collage of traits and behaviours. People aren't robots, though many behave as if they are. The few interesting ones are contradictory, so I paint word pictures of them. Character doodles. This was the one I did for Mary.

MARY KING

Working class. Intellectually aspirational.

Something happened to stifle her dreams – Marriage? Pregnancy? Some sort of failure, perhaps in exams? Trauma – parent or loved one dying? From this moment: quiet rage; determination to make life pay.

Bored with husband. He represents second best. She the do-er, him the braggart. She leads. He follows. The romance of money beckons and the dream of Fiji.

Obsession with acquiring skills, perhaps in the hope of money: accounting, digital technology. She learns quickly – the speed and determination of the self-taught.

How did she learn to shoot so well? Local rifle club? Weekend territorial stint? Garroting – how did she become so strong? I should have registered the gym bag – her need to be fit.

She learns the kinds of things she wanted her husband to know when he got offered the Ocean Investment job: weapons, technology, phone hacking, so she is re-inventing him, he's almost an alter ego for her and she is both partners in the marriage. When he is killed she becomes the man warrior, the hunter, the killer, the vengeful God. The murders are the fulfilment of a mission and assuagement of guilt. Beneath this she keeps the conventional woman part of her character intact – blonde, red dress, flirtation. She is becoming increasingly Jekyll and Hyde, a series of characters rather than a personality.

NATURAL LAW – this concept gives her intellectual and moral justification for her killing sprees.

GLADIATOR – she adopts Symon's codename in the hope that I will find him.

Conflates a return to order with personal revenge. This is the behaviour of a true psychotic.

The more I added the more interesting and deadly she became. I knew she would have left her home but I all I had to do was keep my phone online and wait. I finished, gave Alfred a cuttlefish and some raisins and left. Getting out of the university was like trying to escape from a Stalag. Audrey Pritchard was stalking the corridors wearing what looked like a bacofoil wrapping. I wondered if it was some strange metaphor about the abuse of poultry.

"Before you say anything, Audrey – next Tuesday, my room at 4 pm. You can make your complaint in detail and I will challenge you in kind."

She looked at me smugly. She clearly had a small bomb to drop.

"Ronald Coombes is in hospital. He made a suicide attempt. He keeps saying he only wants to talk to you. Sometimes I think you are not just incompetent and workshy but also dangerous to know, Dr. Rook," she said.

*

The hospital looked like a large block of flats. We all hate them, because they remind us of our own mortality. Soiled bandages, the organs creak, swell, go-slow working, channels narrow, pipes clog, things distend or diminish, routines become unruly, ordinary functions are painful and humiliating, dreams come thick and fast until a storm of fading bleaches them, the last cough, the dissolution of thought and the fading of being, words like weaken, fail, deterioration are the vocabulary of ordinary death.

In contrast to this gloomy rendering of my thoughts, Ron sat up in bed, a drip attached, eating a Mars Bar with an unpleasant relish. He looked ashen, his eyes like over-chlorinated marbles. He smiled at me.

"I went to Roxanne. She seemed nice. But..."

"You couldn't get it up," I said.

"No. She tried a variety of quite imaginative stimulations. But not even a whimper, let alone a bang. It was the final straw really. So I went home, had a half bottle of Australian chardonnay and a few codeine for my headache. Then I thought: sod it, and I took the lot.

"Ron. It's all my fault. I'm so sorry."

"No, no, I want to thank you. It's the best thing that's ever happened to me."

I was surprised. He looked blissfully ill.

"I'm off work for three months on full pay. I'm going to have intensive one to one therapy with a psychiatrist, *gratis*, and they're putting me in a self-help group as soon as my liver's recovered. One of the Nurses said there are five women to every man in the group. So...life couldn't be better really."

I took his hand and shook it.

"I'm very happy for you, Ron."

Chapter XXI

'It is the dim haze of mystery that adds enchantment to pursuit.'

Antoine Rivarol

My phone beeped earlier than I thought. She must have moved quickly. It was 10 a.m. the next day. I guessed that meant that she would have dropped her children off the night before. It would give her better cover travelling with them, but it also put them at risk and it would slow her down. I put a few things in my pocket, grabbed a slice of toast and went out to my car. I turned on the laptop to get a better visual reading. Mary's biological tracking device slipped in my coffee was a lot higher up the techno pecking order than mine, but the one I had put beneath the Little Pony sticker on her laptop when we first met was still working. Ironically I did it because she felt she was in danger and I thought it might come in useful to know where she was. I hadn't told her because I didn't want to frighten her.

She was driving south. I was no more than fifty minutes behind her. My guess was Heathrow or Gatwick and given that I was pretty sure she was leaving the country – the dream of Fiji beckoned – she would have luggage to check in, so unless she was really playing with margins or running very late I would have time.

*

Heathrow. I checked the airlines. I bought a newspaper, sat and waited. The tracking device was still happily bleating a faint orange light on my phone. Luggage was checked in, goodbyes were being exchanged. A trim woman with black hair, wearing a two piece pin stripe designer suit, clipped past with some expensive luggage on wheels. I wasn't fooled. I would know those legs anywhere. I stepped in front of her as she looked in her bag for her travel documents.

"We can't go on meeting like this," I said.

Her eyes flickered and, just for a moment, she thought of bluffing it out and forcing me to make a scene, but she was too intelligent, and smiled. I took out the hair in the tiny plastic envelope and showed it to her.

"Anna took a souvenir. The police will have found others and this will match."

She looked annoyed rather than frightened.

"Why can't you let it go? I disappear and you never hear from me again. You're no friend to the police and you're not some bloody *Daily Mail* moralist. Or perhaps you are and the shambolic free thinking philosopher mask is just that – a pose you strike to impress gullible students. Are you just a paper tiger?"

"You'll have to dig a lot deeper than that if you want to wound me. It's Anna. I owe it to her."

She looked at me derisively.

"You told me I confused a sense of mission with personal guilt over Andy's death. That's exactly what you're doing with Anna."

"The difference is – I know it," I said. "I'm making a pathetic attempt at redress and perhaps even making myself feel marginally better, though that rarely works. Come on, Mary. I'm not letting you go. It's also professional pride. You set me up."

Something happened to her then, a transformation. Five hundred years ago I would have believed it to be a possession. Her pupils widened and darkened. Blue eyes became black, the whites shone, as if she was a shape changer. She moved in close to me as if she couldn't decide whether to kiss or bite me. Lavender and almonds and a whiff of insanity.

"All my life I've met men who are losers. Who can't hack it. Who aren't my equal. Years ago, when I heard you talking in that lecture hall, I thought I'd met someone better. But you're all wind and straw. Hollow man."

"That's me," I said.

"But what you've got to ask yourself, Paul, is: what is she holding against my ribs? A nail file, or a knife? One big enough to get between the bone and stop the heart."

It was a good question. I felt the tip of something against my chest. I leaned forward until I was almost kissing her eyelids. I bent down and whispered into her left ear.

"Go on then. Push. Do it."

She looked at me. I felt the sharpness increase. She was clinically insane. Perhaps even she knew it. She smiled.

"Paul, come away with me. We could have such a life. I have money. You can do what you like with me and I'll enjoy it. My kids can follow. They'll adore you."

She was so close. A world of macabre possibilities opened in my mind. A door had opened. The Marquis de Sade would have run through it. But I was Paul Rook, monumental fuck up. I had my darling Cass, Anna to avenge, a failed academic career to pursue, scores to settle, vanities to unravel, pomposities to prick, David to destroy, Lizzie to love hopelessly. How could I turn my back on such a life feast?

"It's over, Mary."

She clicked her tongue against the roof of her mouth as if she had just lost a small bet, stepped back and put the nail file in her handbag.

"Ok," she said, defeated. "But you take me in. At least I can embarrass your reputation by making you deal with the police."

We walked towards the exit. She suddenly stopped.

"Tell me, now it doesn't matter. Did you find me attractive?"

I took a deep breath.

"I've woken up several times with you on my mind and a thundering erection under the duvet. Small childlike hands capable of killing and depravity, eyes set on impossible horizons, pale skin to madden all men, legs to die in the Crusades for. You are dangerously sexy."

"It was all worth it, then," she said coquettishly. She looked at the Ladies room. "I need to go and take off this stupid wig and put on some make up. I'm not going to be arrested looking like a library card."

I asked a cleaner if there was any other exit from the Ladies and she said there wasn't. I told Mary she had two minutes. Two minutes later I realised how stupid I'd been and went inside. One locked cubicle. I entered the one next to it and stood on the seat to look over. Mary sitting on the toilet, her upper body sideways against the wall, a thin garrotte tightened around her throat. I got down and shoved my shoulder against the cubicle door. It gave way easily and I almost fell on her. The black wig askew, the tongue already swelling horribly through the lips. Mary King and her train of destruction and mayhem was no more. Two more motherless children in the world. It must take a will of iron to garrotte yourself.

I left the Ladies and put a chair across the door to suggest it was closed. I couldn't risk a phone call until I was clear of the airport, so some poor soul would have to discover Mary's body. So many things had happened in the past week to incriminate me in various ways I was amazed the police had not already been to see me. As I walked towards the terminal exit someone bumped into me and we both stopped. He stared at me. It was the American who had followed me to Prague.

"My fault entirely," he said. "Is everything OK? All done?"

"All done," I said.

He half smiled.

"Am I OK to walk away too?" I asked.

He looked around. Two armed policemen were strolling through.

"Of course," he said. "Life goes on." He nodded and walked away. CIA? Ocean Investments? Political trouble-shooter? God alone knew and He wasn't telling me anything. He never did. But I was safe from any police investigation, I did understand that much. I had no illusions – it was precisely because I was of no consequence that I was safe. Any connection with Anna's death they discovered might lead to me saying something awkward for the big players in this dirty game of money and guns, so a phone call or a word in a bar or at a club, and it's all hushed. If I was more important I'd be in more danger. The irony wasn't lost on me.

Chapter XXII

'No human thing is of serious importance'
Plato

4 p.m. Tuesday. Audrey knocked and entered, followed by the Registrar, a slow-witted man with too many teeth and a nasal whine of a voice, and two pro vice chancellors, Tweedledum and Tweedledee. Audrey looked around, surprised at so many people. There were some fifteen students, including the President of the SU, a feisty young woman called Haneefah. Cass was among them. Alfred sat on my desk eating a plum and eyeing Audrey suspiciously. Mrs Simpson sat in an easy chair with a mug of tea.

"Dr. Rook, this is a formal disciplinary meeting, not a bingo hall," Audrey said.

"It's also a democracy. You have your representative, I have a number of mine, and given that I am making a counter complaint to your complaint I can have who the hell I like here."

I was playing to the gallery and the gallery liked it. She couldn't back down without it looking like a defeat, so she sat, with Toothy next to her, and the pro vice chancellors bookending them. Toothy read her complaint, which amounted to me being guilty of gross misconduct and several counts of an "unreasonable refusal to carry out a reasonable instruction." The removal of Alfred was one of these. If found guilty I could be sacked. I disputed every count and immediately countered with an accusation that she exceeded her authority, had proven herself incompetent, and moved that we needed a new head of department. Audrey smiled.

"Dr Rook, if you wish to put yourself forward for the position of head of department, then may I suggest…"

"Oh, I'm not, Professor. I'm thinking of a far more suitable candidate altogether."

She looked discombobulated. Tweedledum and Tweedledee looked at each other and Toothy looked determinedly at his crotch. I let the moment hang.

"I move that we have a democratic vote on a new *de facto* interim head of department until such time as the whole faculty is present for a full debate."

"Who are you suggesting, Dr Rook?" asked Toothy, genuinely curious.

I produced my trump card.

"I suggest Alfred," I said. "The parrot."

"I second that," said Cass.

Everyone's eyes swivelled to Alfred, who sensed that he had an audience and did a little jig on the desk. I had a few key words which I knew would trigger him into action if required.

"You're utterly mad!" said Audrey.

"Foucault argues that madness…" I began and Alfred picked up the rest, "…that madness is silenced by reason, thereby losing its power to highlight the limits of social order and to point to uncomfortable truths."

The mouths of several students and certainly those of Tweedledum and Tweedledee dropped several inches. I gave Alfred a grape.

"Into the valley of death rode the six hundred," he said.

Everyone sensed a genuine drama. Where would this end? I had the initiative, or rather Alfred did, so I decided to push home the advantage.

"I propose Alfred because he is liked and respected by the student population, and because he is clearly a scholar with a wide conceptual grasp of the history of ideas. On Natural Law for example."

Alfred blinked his onyx-black eyes and commenced a discourse in a dazzling compendium of different voices: "Natural law is often conflated with common law, but the two are distinct in that natural law is a view that certain rights or values are universally inherent in or cognizable by virtue of human reason or human nature, 'ave a juicy grape, darlin', while common law is the legal tradition whereby certain rights or values are legally cognizable, *cannon to the left of them, cannon to the right,* by virtue of judicial recognition or articulation... " He stopped to eat a grape from my hand. Three students applauded, then the others joined in, and one, a mop-haired scarecrow with a bobble hat, punched the air and shouted, "You the man, bro!"

"I suppose he publishes too," said Audrey.

I frowned and shook my head at her.

"Professor Pritchard, you may have noticed that Alfred is differently bodied, and therefore typing is a problem. I thought that as a university we were committed to equality, diversity, and provision for the differently abled?"

"Yo!" said a thin white girl who imagined herself a Harlem street radical.

"I told you to get rid of that disgusting bird!" said Audrey.

"Moving a parrot from its home is what a fascist would do," said Cass.

"I'm not a fascist just for trying to get a bloody parrot off campus," said Audrey, her voice a tremor of outrage.

"Not fascist but species-ist. Which is almost fascist," said the bobble hat.

"Quasi fascist," said a young girl with purple pigtails and a hat like an apple pie.

"Neo-Nazi," said a young boy, his ears bolted with wing nuts.

"I am neither a Nazi nor a fascist," said Audrey. "Your argument is completely specious."

"Just what a Neo-Nazi would say," said Haneefah. The others cheered.

Two crimson spots appeared on Audrey's cheeks. The cracks had appeared and were rending. The battle wasn't over but the war was won. I sat back and watched the chaos with a deep, soul-warming delight. The outcome was some ludicrous compromise whereby another meeting would be called to discuss the ramifications of this meeting. It would all evaporate.

*

Half an hour later Cass and I were giggling our way across the car park. A little anarchic madness had been timely to dispel the horror and sadness of the past week. I put my arm around her.

"You will be sacked, you know," she said.

"I live in hope, my darling. Alfred's perfectly capable of teaching philosophy, so you'll be OK."

"When I was little, I thought that basically everything was stable, fixed, and I could have a tantrum every now and then, but things would always return to normal. Now I think normal is chaos."

"Welcome to my world. Let's go for a pizza."

Chapter XXIII

'Human kind cannot bear very much reality.'

T.S. Eliot

To avoid madness it is necessary to order things. That night Cass and I opened a bottle of Sancerre, lit a candle, and toasted Symon. I read a few lines of Baudelaire which I know he liked.

I greet

the desert and the sea with tenderness:

I laugh at funerals, I cry at feasts,

wine tastes smooth that's full of bitterness

We had a quiet evening. For once I slept like an angel. At dawn I drove to a favourite place. A walk past a giant elm whose indifference always reassures me that there are bigger things at work than the small lunacies of human beings, to a stream that forks into the river Avon. I sat on the bank, dangling my legs almost in the water. The current was fast and the sound of the water made me imagine the whisperings of the dead. I took the tiny shell from my pocket, kissed it and threw it in the stream. It bubbled and rippled for an instant and was gone. The sun glittered the water. I said sorry, but the word was thin, and then from out of the air came a song, the one song that I remembered Anna saying she loved. *As Time Goes By*. She sang it once. I hummed the melody and a few words, "a smile is just a smile, a kiss is just a kiss, as time goes by…" and then I left.

*

I drove straight to my Mum's. She was sitting staring into space, seeing God knows what. I kissed her forehead, the skin thin and papery, then sat and held her bony hands in mine. I decided I would stop treating her like a ghost, and would tell her real things.

"You liked Symon coming, didn't you, Mum? He loved seeing you. Afraid he won't be able to any more, but I'll come more often, and I'm sorry I've neglected you a bit."

Something in her stirred.

"Nice lad, Symon. Cupcake Symon. Made me think, that boy." And she smiled. A lovely resonant smile. I stayed another half an hour, and then rose to leave. She opened a drawer and took out a crumpled heap of papers, and made a 'Shhh' gesture. I played along and pocketed them, then kissed her and left. In my car I took out the papers and straightened them on the passenger seat. They were her scrawly drawings of weird creatures, except now I really looked, I could see something else. These weren't just phantoms, they were letters. The wings of a harpy were the cross in a T. A gaping mouth was a P. An insect-like horror was an E. Another the same. I straightened them all and fifteen minutes later I had a name. Pete James. It was the only possible combination that made sense. I knew exactly what she'd given me. The name of my father. I almost gagged on my own tears. Why did it mean so much? But it did, it just did. And now I would try to find him.

Printed in Great Britain
by Amazon